Harstairs House

AMANDA GRANGE

BERKLEY SENSATION, NEW YORK

THE BERKLEY PUBLISHING GROUP
Published by the Penguin Group
Penguin Group (USA) Inc.
375 Hudson Street, New York, New York 10014, USA
Penguin Group (Canada), 90 Eglinton Avenue East, Suite 700, Toronto, Ontario M4P 2Y3, Canada
(a division of Pearson Penguin Canada Inc.)
Penguin Books Ltd., 80 Strand, London WC2R 0RL, England
Penguin Group Ireland, 25 St. Stephen's Green, Dublin 2, Ireland (a division of Penguin Books Ltd.)
Penguin Group (Australia), 250 Camberwell Road, Camberwell, Victoria 3124, Australia
(a division of Pearson Australia Group Pty. Ltd.)
Penguin Books India Pvt. Ltd., 11 Community Centre, Panchsheel Park, New Delhi—110 017, India
Penguin Group (NZ), 67 Apollo Drive, Rosedale, North Shore 0632, New Zealand
(a division of Pearson New Zealand Ltd.)
Penguin Books (South Africa) (Pty.) Ltd., 24 Sturdee Avenue, Rosebank, Johannesburg 2196, South
Africa

Penguin Books Ltd., Registered Offices: 80 Strand, London WC2R 0RL, England

HARSTAIRS HOUSE

Copyright © 2004 by Amanda Grange
Cover art by Aleta Rafton
Cover design by George Long
Text design by Tiffany Estreicher

First American edition: December 2007
Originally published in Great Britain by Robert Hale Ltd. in 2004.

Berkley Sensation trade paperback ISBN: 978-0-425-21773-3

PRINTED IN THE UNITED STATES OF AMERICA

10 9 8 7 6 5 4 3 2 1

CHAPTER ONE

Miss Susannah Thorpe looked out at the dismal November morning in the year of 1793 and sighed. The dull sky had leeched the colour from the gardens and reduced them to a dreary shade of grey. A few last leaves, clinging to the trees, were drenched by the pouring rain. At least when she had been appointed as a governess to the Russell children it had been the start of summer, and the warm, sunny weather had allowed her to take them into the garden. But today, for the tenth day in succession, they would be confined to the schoolroom, which meant their behaviour would be dreadful.

The clock struck the hour. She wrapped a shawl round her shoulders and tidied her mouse-brown hair, then made her way to the schoolroom. The children were already there, being supervised by their nurse, Mrs. Hitchins, who smiled benignly as Master Thomas pulled Miss Isabelle's pigtails. "'E's a proper boy, 'e is," said Mrs. Hitchins indulgently, as she passed Susannah on her way out of the room.

He's a proper monster, thought Susannah, but did not say so. She knew that anything she said to the nurse would be reported to Mrs. Russell, and such a remark could easily lead to her being dismissed.

Master David, meanwhile, was kicking Master Julian, who was about to retaliate by pouring ink over his brother's head. Susannah prayed for patience then set about restoring order. She coaxed the children to their desks and then she handed out their slates. As soon as she handed one to Master David, he drew his fingernails across it and smiled with glee as a ghastly screeching noise filled the schoolroom. When Master Julian decided to copy him, Susannah prepared herself for yet another nerve-jangling day.

Hardly had it begun, however, when the door opened and one of the housemaids entered.

"You're wanted downstairs," the housemaid said to Susannah.

Susannah's spirits sank. What had she done this time? The children were forever bearing tales, and she was constantly being reprimanded for imaginary grievances.

"You'd better 'urry," said the maid.

"What about the children?" asked Susannah.

The boys were already flicking pieces of chalk across the room.

"I'm to stay with 'em until you get back," said the house-maid warily.

Master David whooped with glee, whilst Master Julian began pulling faces at the hapless girl.

Susannah might be going to receive a scold, but she was beginning to think she would rather face one of Mrs. Russell's tirades than deal with the children's unruly behaviour.

How had it come to this? she thought, as she descended the stairs and then crossed the hall. Two years before, she had been a happy young lady from a poor but respectable family. Her mother having died at her birth, her father had raised her in a small cottage by the sea, but when she was eleven he, too, had died, and she had been raised by her Great Aunt Caroline. Time had taken its toll, and Great Aunt Caroline had at last passed away, leaving Susannah alone in the world. A post as a companion had followed, but when her elderly employer had emigrated, Susannah had been forced to seek another position, this time as a governess in the Russell household.

She paused outside the drawing-room door to straighten her skirt, then she knocked on the door and Mrs. Russell's querulous voice called, "Come in."

She opened the door to reveal a splendid apartment

with gold-painted walls, a marble fireplace carved with two female figures, and a collection of damask chairs and sofas. Lying in front of the fireplace on a chaise longue, dressed in an enchanting gown of gold silk, was Mrs. Russell. Having convinced herself that she was delicate, Mrs. Russell spent her days moving from her bed to her chaise longue and back again in a never-ending cycle of bodily inactivity, so that her mind was free to find fault with everyone and everything about her.

"What took you so long?" asked Mrs. Russell, in a peevish voice. "Mr. Sinders has been waiting for you for ten minutes. Really, girl, you should know better than to dawdle when you are sent for. Other people's time is valuable, even if yours is not."

Mr. Sinders raised his eyebrows at this speech, but said nothing except, "How do you do, Miss Thorpe."

"How do you do," said Susannah, eyeing him cautiously.

Mr. Sinders was an elderly man with the look of a doctor or other professional person about him. His clothes were smart, but not smart enough to threaten his employers' superiority by being too well cut, or made of too fine a cloth. His tailcoat was black with large gilt buttons and his knee breeches were tucked into white stockings. On his feet he wore black shoes.

"Mr. Sinders has come all the way from London to see

you," said Mrs. Russell. "You might at least seem pleased to see him."

A look of distaste crossed Mr. Sinders's face at Mrs. Russell's renewed ill humour.

"May we have somewhere private to discuss our business?" he asked.

"Anything you have to say to Miss Thorpe may be said in front of me," Mrs. Russell declared.

"Unfortunately, I'm not at liberty to discuss the matter with anyone else," said Mr. Sinders firmly.

Mrs. Russell's mouth set in a petulant line.

"I am not anyone else: I am Miss Thorpe's employer, and naturally I take a motherly interest in her welfare," she said.

Mr. Sinders raised his eyebrows at this blatant lie, but he did not contradict Mrs. Russell. Instead, he said, "Nevertheless, I am bound by my profession to honour Mr. Harstairs's edicts."

He spoke politely, but there was a note of steel in his voice, and it told Susannah he would not be swayed.

"Very well," said Mrs. Russell peevishly. "Morton, show Mr. Sinders to the library, and do hurry up. No, leave your knitting. Whatever that misshapen garment is, it can wait. Go now, at once. And take care you don't bore him to death with your prattle."

Miss Morton, an ageing spinster who had the dubious

pleasure of being Mrs. Russell's companion, sprang to her feet and led the way out of the room, murmuring, "Oh, of course, yes indeed, let me show you the way."

Flustering and fluffing, Miss Morton led Susannah and Mr. Sinders through the hall to the back of the house, where she opened a door into the library. It was a spacious apartment lined with books, and had a buttoned leather sofa set in front of the fireplace. Wing chairs were placed on either side of it, and behind it, tall windows looked out on to the dreary garden.

"Thank you," said Mr. Sinders politely, making Miss Morton a bow.

"Oh, thank *you*," she fluttered, unused to such civil treatment. She smiled nervously at Susannah and then departed, closing the door behind her.

"Won't you be seated?" asked Mr. Sinders.

Susannah sat on the sofa and arranged the folds of her gown to hide a patch on the hem.

"I expect you are wondering who I am," said Mr. Sinders, as he sat down in one of the wing chairs.

"Yes, I am," said Susannah.

"I represent Mr. Harstairs; I am his lawyer."

"I have never heard of Mr. Harstairs," said Susannah.

"Mr. Harstairs was once betrothed to your Great Aunt Caroline," said Mr. Sinders.

Susannah's eyes opened wide in surprise. Great Aunt

Caroline had never mentioned any love affairs, and Susannah had assumed she had passed through life unruffled by its passions.

"I never knew Great Aunt Caroline had been betrothed," she said.

"Once, many years ago. There was a misunderstanding, and the wedding was abandoned. Mr. Harstairs threw himself into his business, going abroad for many years. When he returned he was a wealthy man. He never married and, in short, when he died, he left everything to you."

"To me?" asked Susannah in astonishment.

"Yes, to you."

"But why?"

"You are all that is left of the woman he loved," said Mr. Sinders simply. "I should say, before I go any further, that your inheritance is subject to certain conditions. They are somewhat unusual. In order to claim your inheritance—a large one, I might add; one that would relieve you of the necessity of earning your own living, and allow you to live in comfort for the rest of your life—you must either marry within a month from today, or you must spend a month in Harstairs House."

"That doesn't seem too difficult," said Susannah. "Since I know no gentlemen, and have no intention of marrying a gentleman I don't know, I will not be able to carry out the first option, but I see no difficulty in carrying out the second."

Mr. Sinders pursed his lips and steepled his fingers, then leant back in his chair.

"I should perhaps warn you that Harstairs House is said to be haunted," he remarked.

Susannah laughed. "I have been a governess to the Russell children for three months, two weeks and five days, Mr. Sinders. There is nothing a ghost can do to frighten me after that!"

Mr. Sinders gave a dry smile.

"It does not seem a congenial household," he admitted. "But think carefully. Marriage would be an easier option, and with such a fortune you would be able to have your pick of husbands. If you decide to inhabit Harstairs House, I must tell you that you will be isolated for an entire month, for it is set on a promontory overlooking the Cornish coast. Then there is the fact that you would have to take up residence at once."

"I have nothing to stay here for," said Susannah. She thought for a moment and then said, "If I go to Harstairs House and don't remain for a month, what then?"

"You will be awarded an amount of money for each night you pass there: ten pounds for the first night, twenty for the second night, forty for the third, eighty for the fourth and so on."

"So the longer I stay, the greater my reward," mused Susannah.

"Exactly."

"And if I stay the full month?" she asked.

"Then you will inherit the house, and a fortune of one hundred thousand pounds."

"One hundred . . . ?" Susannah was speechless.

"Thousand pounds," Mr. Sinders finished for her. "There is a coach waiting outside. In order to fulfil the terms of the will, if you choose to spend a month in the house, you must set out today."

Susannah did not need to think about it. Anything must be better than teaching the Russell children for another month. It would either turn her grey or send her to Bedlam!

"May I take someone with me?" she asked.

Mr. Sinders looked surprised.

"I don't know," he said. "There is nothing in the will that says you can't, so yes, I suppose that would be all right. Do you have anyone in mind?"

"I do," said Susannah. She stood up. "I will go and ask her if she would like to join me, and then I will pack. It will not take me long, half an hour at most."

Mr. Sinders stood up, too.

"Then I will await you here. Mr. Harstairs made provision for a hired coach to bring me here, and then to take you down to Cornwall. It is a journey on which I am bound to accompany you, to see you safely installed in the house.

As soon as you are ready, we will drive there together," he said.

~ ~ ~

Half an hour later, Susannah was sitting in a smart coach with a travelling cloak thrown over her gown, feeling overjoyed to have left the Russells behind. She did not know what the future held, but she was sure it must be better than the recent past. She cast her eyes round the coach, which was spacious, and fitted out in the first style. There was a writing desk built into it, and the squabs were made of green leather, perfumed with the smell of polish. The coach was comfortable, being well sprung, and it was pulled by a team of horses who made light work of the miles. On the opposite seat sat Mr. Sinders, and next to Susannah sat Miss Constance Morton.

"So good," said Constance for the tenth time, in a daze. "I don't know what I've done to deserve such good fortune, but thank you, Susannah, from the bottom of my heart."

Susannah had not known whether Constance would agree to the scheme, thinking that a haunted house might be too alarming for her, but she had asked nonetheless. Constance had been extremely kind to her when she had first arrived at the Russells' house, making her feel welcome, and comforting her when Mrs. Russell had been particularly spiteful, and she had wanted to repay that kindness. She smiled as she recalled Constance's face when she had mentioned the idea. It had been a picture! Miss Morton had been startled, and had then flushed pink with pleasure before saying, "I am sure ghosts won't bother me. I will simply sit in a corner with my knitting, and once they have seen I am not to be scared, I am sure they will go away."

"I have not been able to hire any servants," said Mr. Sinders, as the coach rattled on its way. "It might be possible to find someone to work there as winter sets in and other work grows scarce, but for now I am afraid you will have to fend for yourselves."

"Please don't worry about it," said Susannah. "I can cook and clean. In fact, I will enjoy it. It will be nice to have hot meals for a change."

Mr. Sinders looked at her enquiringly.

"My meals were brought up to me on a tray at Mrs. Russell's. The food was always cold by the time it reached me in the nursery," she explained.

"Ah," said Mr. Sinders, nodding. "There will be no such difficulty at Harstairs House."

"Will there be everything we need at the house, linen and such like?"

"Yes, everything is there. It's an old, ramshackle building, but the roof is sound and the chimneys have been swept. The only thing you might find uncomfortable are the draughts. Sudden bursts of cold air can set the doors and windows banging, alarming those who are nervous."

"We will just have to wear our shawls!" Susannah said.

"If you should regret your decision and wish to leave the house, there is a village five miles away. It will not take you much more than an hour to walk the distance. If you do, though, remember you will forfeit your inheritance," said Mr. Sinders.

"And how would you know if we left?" asked Susannah curiously. "If we had a mind to, what is to prevent us from staying the month at a nice, cosy inn and then claiming to have spent it at Harstairs House?"

He gave a dry smile. "Nothing. But if you give me your word you have not left, I will accept it. You are free to wander in the grounds, but if you go through the gate or across the fences, you will lose everything but the allowance for the number of nights you have spent in the house."

"Mr. Harstairs must have been a strange gentleman," said Susannah thoughtfully.

"Mr. Harstairs was something of an eccentric. His eccentricity, combined with the attention to detail he gave to his business matters, made him appear rather odd. But I believe he was quite sane."

As the coach bowled through the country lanes, they fell silent. Susannah tried to imagine the gentleman who had fallen in love with Great Aunt Caroline. He must have loved her a great deal, she reflected, for he had never married, and had left all his possessions to Caroline's great-niece.

She leaned back against the comfortable squabs. It was the first piece of good fortune she had had since Aunt Caroline had taken her in, and she was already looking forward to her inheritance. When the month was over, she meant to enjoy her new-found wealth. London shops, with their silk gowns, lace shawls and fetching hats beckoned her. There would be rides in the park, museums, assemblies. . . . Susannah fell into a happy reverie as the coach travelled south.

~　~　~

It was dark when the coach finally turned off the road and began to make its way down a narrow lane. As it progressed, Susannah heard a faint swishing noise in the distance. It gradually grew louder, and at last she realized that it was the sea!

"Does Harstairs House have a way down to the shore?" she asked Mr. Sinders with interest.

"It does," he replied.

"I haven't seen the sea for years," said Susannah wistfully. "But I don't suppose I will see it tonight."

She peered out of the window, but the moon was obscured by clouds, and the few stars that pierced the blackness could do no more than shed a faint, silvery light on the world below.

"The village is that way," said Mr. Sinders, pointing down an even narrower lane to their left. "It is marked with a signpost, do you see?"

Susannah nodded as the coach rolled past the post. She could just read the word Harding and the number 1¾ by the light of the coach lamps. She made an effort to memorize the way, in case she should need it in the future.

At last the coach slowed and turned into an imposing set of gates a little further up the lane.

"This marks the point beyond which you cannot go," said Mr. Sinders.

The coach wound up a long drive bordered by open ground, and then turned a corner to reveal a huge house. It was the oddest building Susannah had ever seen. It had none of the grace and beauty of Mrs. Russell's home, with its symmetrical façade and tall windows. Instead, it looked as though it had been thrown up by a violent upheaval of the land.

"It used to be a farmhouse," said Mr. Sinders. "When it burned down, its owner restored it and added to it, but he had little use for architects and built for practicality. I am not a connoisseur of such things, but even I can see that it is ugly."

"It's a monstrosity," Susannah agreed.

The house was square, with its front wall being almost as high as it was long. Windows dotted it at irregular intervals, and they were all of different sizes. The door seemed askew, as though it had been blown that way by a particularly fierce wind.

"But it is well built," reflected Mr. Sinders. "The stone is thick, and the windows facing the ocean are small, to protect the rooms from storms. There is a central courtyard which provides some relief from the prevailing wind, and although it is at present overgrown, I'm sure it could be made very pleasant. You might care to walk there if the rain stops."

The drive turned again and the house was lost from view, until it finally reappeared in front of them and the coach rolled to a halt.

"Here I must leave you. I am allowed to go no further," said Mr. Sinders. "You will find the house has been well supplied. Mr. Harstairs's valet has made sure you have everything you need, including food and drink. Fresh supplies of eggs, milk and so forth will be left outside the kitchen door each morning. If you wish to send letters you may do so. The boy who brings the supplies will collect them, and I have made arrangements to have them delivered for you."

"You seem to have thought of everything. I'm sure we'll be very comfortable," she said.

"Is there anything further you wish to ask?" he enquired. "I am not allowed to see you until you emerge from the house, when I will be waiting for you, with a coach to take you to London. If there is anything pressing in the meantime you may write to me and I am allowed to reply; but it would be easier for me to answer any questions you might have now."

Susannah considered. "No, I don't think so," she said.

"Then it remains only for me to give you this," he said, taking a large iron key out of his pocket and handing it to her. "It is for the front door. There is also a key for the kitchen door, which you will find hanging on a hook by the dresser."

Susannah took the key.

"I wish you luck, and now I must bid you goodnight," he said.

The coachman opened the door and let down the step. Susannah climbed out of the coach, followed by Constance, and the two ladies collected their portmanteaux, then set off up the drive. Behind her, Susannah heard the coach turning and then leaving, the clop of the horses' hooves growing fainter and fainter as the coach rolled away.

"It's very big," said Constance faintly, looking at the huge house that sprawled in front of them like a misshapen giant.

"And very dark," said Susannah with a shiver.

"There will be candles inside?" asked Constance hesitantly.

"I'm sure there will be," said Susannah bracingly. "Mr.

Sinders said the house had been equipped with everything we will need."

Now that she had arrived at the house, however, she was not feeling so confident. It was one thing to laugh at ghosts in the daylight when the haunted house was miles away, but it was quite another to laugh at them when the night was dark and wet, and the house in front of her was unknown and forbidding. However, she told herself not to be so lily-livered, and reminding herself that she had Constance for company, she approached the house. In the dim starlight she could see that the door had been painted, but the paint was peeling off. Nevertheless, the porch around it offered some shelter from the elements, and the two ladies stood beneath the canopy as Susannah put the key in the lock. It turned with a hollow click and the door swung open.

It was dark inside. There appeared to be a hall stretching out in front of them, and doors leading off to either side. Susannah went in. She stood still for a few minutes, to let her eyes adjust to the dark. It was so quiet she could hear Constance breathing behind her. Gradually, she began to make out shapes in the hall. There was a table in front of her, and there might be a candlestick on it. She moved forward, and tripped over something. A clattering noise reverberated round the hall, making her jump.

Behind her, Constance said, "Oh!"

Susannah picked herself up and felt all round her,

knowing she had kicked over a stool. She found it, righted it, whispered to Constance to be careful, and went cautiously towards the table. To her relief, she made out the dim outline of a candlestick, complete with candle. Fumbling on the table, her hand closed round a tinder box. She lit the candle, noticing with surprise that her hand trembled slightly as she did so, and then looked about her. The flickering flame revealed a little of the hall. It was about twenty feet square, and had two doors leading off from either side of her. Ahead of her, there were two more doors, with two corridors flanking them and running away from her, into the dark reaches of the house.

The candle flickered fitfully. There were draughts blowing from every direction, threatening to extinguish the flame. Seeing a branched candelabra set on a table pushed against the wall, Susannah went over to it and lit its candles, being reassured by the five flames. She handed the single candlestick to Constance and said, "Follow me."

Gripping her portmanteau, she headed towards one of the doors directly opposite her. As she reached the other side of the hall, however, she started, for a faint light came from the direction of the left-hand corridor, and with a disquieting feeling she thought it came from a candle. But that was nonsense. It must be the moon, shining in through one of the windows. She almost reassured herself, but knowing that she would not be easy until she had made certain, she proceeded down the corridor. If there was a vagrant in the house, she would rather find him now than have him find *her* when she was asleep.

The further she went, the stronger the light became. It was creeping under the door at the end of the corridor. Moreover, she thought she could hear voices. She started to feel uneasy. Suppose the house was really haunted?

Nonsense, she told herself again. Even so, she turned round, beckoning Constance to come and walk beside her . . . and realized that Constance was not there.

Her heart began to thud. Where was Constance? She wanted to call out for the spinster, but she felt suddenly wary. What if unfriendly ears were listening? She turned back towards the door. She would have no peace until she knew what lay behind it, either moonlight or ghosts, and forcing herself forward she went on. If she looked through the keyhole, she would know for sure, without having to reveal her presence to unfriendly eyes.

She had almost reached the door when she heard someone behind her. Turning round, she held the candlestick aloft . . . to see a swarthy face, a lithe body, and hands that caught her wrists and refused to let go.

"Well, well, well, so this is the rat," came a mocking voice.

"Rat?" she demanded, so startled that she stopped trying to squirm out of his grip.

Passing her wrists into one of his large hands, he opened the door with the other and pushed her unceremoniously into the middle of the room. Fleetingly, she took in her surroundings, and saw herself to be in a library lined with book shelves. A large table was littered with paper, and in the middle of it was a cut-glass decanter. Placed around it were three glasses, two of which were half full. There were six chairs, three of which appeared to have been thrust back in a hurry. Candles on the mantelpiece lit the room almost as brightly as day.

"It seems I was wrong. It wasn't a rat making the noise."

"I will thank you not to speak of me like that," said Susannah, eyeing him nervously.

"No? Then how should I speak of you?" he enquired softly. "Burglar, vagrant—or spy?"

CHAPTER TWO

Susannah summoned the memory of years of dealing with tradesmen to her aid. Before she had been ground down by Mrs. Russell, she had been able to hold her own against butchers and bakers who had thought to cheat her because of her youth. "Look them up and down, state your case clearly, and brook no dissent," her Great Aunt Caroline had said, and it was advice that had stood her in good stead.

Looking the unknown gentleman up and down, however, was far more unnerving than casting an eye over a portly butcher. He was some eight inches taller than she was, making him over six feet tall, and his shoulders seemed to fill the room. The state of his dress was even more alarming—or undress, as it could more truthfully be called. He was wearing nothing but a ruffled shirt, unbuttoned down to his navel, a pair of leather breeches, and top boots that were dull and stained with hard use. Added to this was his uncompromising visage, with sharp cheekbones, a chin that looked as though it had been quarried and a dark mouth that cut an uncompromising line across his face. His eyes, by contrast, were like jewels, glittering hard and blue from underneath his dark brows, and long dark hair spilled in untidy waves over his shoulders. Nevertheless, she had to speak.

"What have you done with Constance?" she said.

His eyes narrowed.

"So there are two of you."

"Constance is my companion," said Susannah. "I want to know what you have done with her—in fact, I want you to return her to me, now."

"I don't have time for games," he said, ignoring her demands. "I want to know what you are doing here."

"Return Constance to me and I might tell you," said Susannah firmly.

She was outwardly brave, but she was inwardly alarmed. The three glasses on the table told their own tale, and she was afraid that the other two gentlemen would soon return. And then another thought hit her. What if the other two gentlemen were at that very minute tying up Constance in some dark corner of the house?

"If you don't return my companion to me at once, I will . . ."

"You will what?" he asked.

". . . I will report you to the authorities," she said defiantly.

"*I* am the authority in this house," he returned.

"You? You're nothing but an interloper. I am the one who will inherit the house. What's more, my lawyer knows I am here, so if you think you can murder me without anyone knowing, then you're mistaken."

She sidled towards the door as she spoke, hoping to step out into the corridor. She thought he hadn't spotted her casual movement, and continued to move slowly across the room, until a casual movement of his own put him in her path.

"I will ask you again, what are you doing here?" he demanded.

As she could see no other way of leaving the room, she decided unwillingly that she must explain. Once he knew the circumstances, he would surely let her go.

"I am here to claim my inheritance," she said. "I have to spend a month in the house, and as long as I do so, it is mine."

"An unlikely tale," he said, with a twist of his mouth.

"Perhaps you would like to tell me yours, then I can tell you how unlikely *that* is," she said scathingly.

"Very well. I have rented the house until the end of the month. I am its tenant."

"Oh." She let out a sigh of relief. "That explains it! Mr. Sinders must have brought me to the wrong house. I beg your pardon. I am seeking Harstairs House. Perhaps you could give me directions?"

"You don't need any. This *is* Harstairs House."

"Then you cannot be the tenant! Mr. Sinders made no mention of it, and I am sure he would have told me if I was to share the house with anyone. I warn you, if any harm comes to me, your crime will be discovered. Mr. Sinders is going to call at the house each day, to see if there is anything I need, and if I am not here he will raise the alarm," she said, with more imagination than truth.

He said nothing, but there was a slight change in his expression and she thought he was cursing inwardly. She felt heartened. For the first time in the encounter she felt she had the upper hand.

"Now," she said. "Where is Constance?"

His stance seemed to relax a little. His shoulders lost the look of cliffs and settled into the softer look of hills instead.

"I have no idea," he said.

"She was right behind me," said Susannah firmly.

"I saw no one but you."

"Then I had better go and look for her."

"First of all, we need to come to some arrangement," he said. "We cannot both occupy the house—"

"I'm glad you've seen sense."

"—but as I have only one month left on my lease, you may occupy it once I have left. I will escort you to the village and you can return in a month's time."

"No. I have to stay now. If I don't, I will inherit nothing."

"I have only your word for it that you are really the heiress of this extraordinary will," he remarked.

"And I have only your word for it that you are really the tenant," she returned, "but if you really refuse to leave, I suggest we share the house. It is big enough. Constance and I can have one wing, and you can have another."

He looked at her long and hard and then said, "No. That will not do."

"Then I suggest you find another solution. I have had a long journey, I'm tired, I'm hungry, I'm worried about my companion, and I have already made one perfectly sensible suggestion. If you don't like it, then you must think of another."

So saying she moved past him and walked over to the door, and to her relief, he let her go.

"Make sure you don't leave the house," he said threateningly.

"I wouldn't dream of it," she retorted. "If I do, I lose everything."

Then she left the room, relieved to be away from him, and went in search of Constance.

~ ~ ~

Once her footsteps had died away down the corridor, the gentleman went over to one of the bookcases. It had seven shelves of varying heights ranging from floor to ceiling. The top and bottom three shelves were full of books, but the middle one displayed a large marble bust. It was of a man with a noble brow and classical profile, and around his head was a wreath of laurel. The gentleman turned the bust. There was a click, and a section of bookcase sprang back to reveal a hidden passage.

"You can come out now," he said.

Two gentlemen, one about thirty years of age and the other of about sixty years, emerged. They, too, were partially dressed, with ruffled shirts over leather breeches.

"Well done, Oliver," said the older of the two men.

He was some six inches shorter than Oliver, but sturdily built, with grizzled hair swept back into a queue. His brown eyes were intelligent, and his jaw was determined.

"Did you manage to hear everything?" asked Oliver. "Edward?"

"Yes," said the older man.

"And you, James?"

"Yes," he agreed.

He was almost as tall as Oliver, but had a slight build, with narrow shoulders and long, lean legs. His shoulder-length fair hair was secured at the nape of his neck, and his eyes were green.

"What do you think?"

James spoke. "She could be Harstairs's heir, but I'm not convinced she's telling the truth."

"You think Duchamp might have sent her, and that he's tracked us down?" asked Oliver.

"I think it's possible. We've been here nearly six months now."

"We've kept to ourselves," Oliver pointed out.

"I know. But Kelsey has been seen in the village, getting supplies, and we ourselves go there from time to time. We might have put it about that you have leased the house whilst you look round for an estate you want to buy, but it doesn't mean we've been believed. And even if we have, Duchamp would be bound to send someone to investigate if he heard of strangers moving into a remote house on the coast."

They fell silent, thinking.

At last Oliver spoke.

"I'm inclined to believe her. If Duchamp had sent someone to spy on us, he'd have sent a beauty, someone to seduce us and learn our sailing times when we lowered our defences. But she was plain," he said, recalling her nondescript brown hair and unremarkable face, with neither brilliant eyes nor luscious lips to recommend it. "There was nothing seductive or coquettish about her. What's more, she was frightened. When I grasped her wrist, I felt her tremble. Any woman sent by Duchamp would be used to dangerous situations, and wouldn't have turned a hair."

"Hm," said Edward. "You might be right. Even so, I'd be happier if we could send her away. The last thing we need is a couple of strangers in the house right now."

He took his place at the table and leant back on his chair, so that only two of its legs remained in contact with the floor.

"I don't think we're going to be able to do that," said James. He sat at the end of the table and picked up his glass. "At least, not if she is who she says she is. And even if we could send her away, I think we'd be wise not to. If she spoke about the incident to any of the locals then it would draw attention to our presence here, and that is exactly what we are trying to avoid."

"Agreed," said Edward. "Besides, if she's a spy, I'd rather keep her here where we can see her, instead of letting her go so that she can report on what she's seen."

"As to that, what has she seen?" asked James. "Nothing of any importance."

"I don't agree. She's seen a table set with three wine

glasses in a room containing only one man," said Edward, pursing his lips. "It might start her thinking."

"That was sloppy," agreed James, chagrined. "We should have taken them with us. But we can't change it now."

"Do we let her stay?" Edward asked him.

"Yes," said James.

"I think so, too," said Oliver. "It's the safest option—as long as we keep a close watch on her, and stay alert. What do you think to her idea of sharing the house?"

"It's the best we're likely to come up with. If she has the west wing, we will never see her and, more importantly, she will never see us."

"And if she does by any chance find out what we're doing here?"

"We'll deal with that problem when we come to it." Edward shrugged. "For now, I suggest you tell her you agree to share the house."

Oliver nodded. "And whilst I'm about it, I'll tell her I have friends staying with me. She must have noticed the glasses, and I don't want to make a mystery out of them. She probably thinks you were searching the house, looking for the cause of the noise."

"Agreed. But you'd better fasten your shirt before you go," said Edward. "The companion won't think much of letting you occupy the same house as her young mistress if she sees you looking like that."

Oliver buttoned his shirt and threw a tailcoat over it, then asked with a wolfish smile, "Do I look respectable?"

"Never that," said Edward wryly. "But at least you should avoid giving the companion palpitations."

~ ~ ~

Susannah hurried along the corridor, back to the hall. What could have happened to Constance? she thought anxiously. Constance had been just behind her when they had entered the house, and Susannah had assumed she had followed her down the corridor, but she could not now remember when she had last seen or heard her. She knew Constance had been there in the hall, because she remembered handing her a candlestick, but after that, had she seen or heard her at all?

She emerged into the large, square space of the hall and stopped. She put down her portmanteau and protected her flickering candle flames with her hand. The hall looked eerie. It had not struck her as forcibly when she had been with Constance, but now the corners seemed darker, and the shadows cast by the candlelight seemed grotesque. Telling herself not to be fanciful, she jumped when she heard a creaking noise from the stairs. She looked up. She could just see the staircase outlined in the moonlight that fell through the large window on the landing, but there was no one on it. The noise was nothing more than the old house settling.

Great Aunt Caroline's house had done the same, and she knew she would soon grow used to the sounds.

She looked in every direction, but could see nothing to help her decide which way to go. Constance could be anywhere. Taking a firmer grip on her candlestick, she went over to the first door. It creaked loudly as she thrust it back. She went in, finding herself in a large, rectangular room. There was a dining-table and chairs, a heavy sideboard and long, thick curtains which were drawn back from the windows, revealing a courtyard beyond. Bathed in moonlight, the courtyard had a ghostly appearance. It was overgrown, and criss-crossed with paths. At its centre was a sundial.

She closed the door and tried the next one, finding herself in a sitting-room. A harp stood in one corner, and a threadbare sofa was flanked by two armchairs, which were set in front of an inglenook fireplace. On the wall hung a variety of paintings in heavy gold frames which glinted in the candlelight, but in the dark their scenes were no more than a blur.

Closing the door, she moved on and came to the corridor that mirrored the one she had taken earlier, leading away from the hall. She was about to pass it by when she caught sight of a ghostly will-o'-the-wisp coming towards her down the corridor. It floated eerily in the darkness and her heart skipped a beat—until she realized that it was nothing more alarming than a candle, and that its strange floating movement was caused by it being set on a tray. She smiled, and her anxiety left her. Constance was carrying the tray towards her, and had evidently been making tea!

"Oh, what a relief! I thought I had lost you," said Constance, as the two ladies began to laugh with the release of tension. "I was following you across the hall when I thought I heard something and went to investigate. It was only the creaking of the house, but when I tried to find my way back to you I must have become lost. I was sure I'd seen you take the corridor, but as I went further and further along it I saw no sign of you. I was about to give up and turn back when I saw steps leading downward. I was overcome with a longing for a dish of tea. Hoping the steps led to the kitchen, I took them. I found everything we will need. In fact the kitchen seems to be very well stocked, and the fire is ablaze. You will think me fanciful, but it does not seem as though it is deserted. If I didn't know better, I would think it had been used only a few hours ago."

"It probably had!" said Susannah.

She opened the door into the sitting-room, and led the way inside. Setting her portmanteau down beside the sofa, she lit the candles on the mantelpiece from the ones she had in her hand. As they sprang into life Susannah saw that the sofa was a dull green in colour, and that the paintings on the wall showed scenes of the cliff tops.

She shivered. "It's cold," she said.

"A hot drink will help," said Constance.

They sat on the sofa and Constance poured the tea.

"Well, this is an exciting day and no mistake," said Constance, as she handed a cup to Susannah. "But what did you mean about the kitchen being used?"

Susannah took a sip of the hot tea and felt revived.

"We are not alone in the house," she said.

Constance froze with her cup halfway to her lips.

"You mean there are ghosts here after all?" she gasped.

"No, not ghosts," said Susannah. "Men."

Constance put her cup down with a clatter. "Oh, my!"

"It seems Harstairs House has a tenant."

"What is his name? Is he a gentleman?" asked Constance.

"As to his name, I didn't ask and he did not offer it. As to being a gentleman"—a memory of open shirt, broad chest, worn boots and a swarthy face jumped into her mind—"he is nothing of the kind."

"Oh, my!" said Constance again.

"He is staying here until his lease expires at the end of the month."

"That's most unfortunate," said Constance, with a shake of her grey head. "And most strange," she added. "Mr. Harstairs must have known the house had a tenant when he made his will. I wonder why he wanted you to share it?"

"I can only think he did not expect to die so soon," said Susannah. "The lease has only a month to run."

"It must be as you say. But why did Mr. Sinders not mention it? Mr. Harstairs's valet stocked the house, he said. He must have known there was a gentleman here."

"Perhaps the valet did not tell him," said Susannah thoughtfully.

It did seem rather strange, though.

"Unless . . ." Constance went pink.

Susannah looked at her enquiringly.

"What was the gentleman . . . man . . . like?" she asked.

"Tall and swarthy," said Susannah. "Rude and over-bearing," she added.

"But young?" asked Constance.

"Oh, yes. About eight-and-twenty, I should guess. Why?"

"Well," said Constance hesitantly. "Mr. Harstairs was a romantic. He never forgot your great aunt. Perhaps he hoped . . . perhaps he thought . . . perhaps he wanted you to marry the tenant."

"*Marry the tenant?*" exclaimed Susannah. "Why would Mr. Harstairs want me to do that? Anyway, I have no desire to marry, and if I did, I wouldn't marry the tenant if my life depended on it! I can think of nothing–"

There was a knock at the door. Susannah and Constance looked at each other.

"Come in," called Susannah.

The door opened to reveal the man they had just been talking about. Susannah felt a flush spring to her cheeks as she wondered if he could have overheard their conversation, but she was reassured to see that he did not seem annoyed or out of countenance. Regaining her composure, she said, "Yes?"

"I hope I'm not intruding?" he asked.

"No, not at all," fluttered Constance, putting down her cup.

He was now properly dressed, Susannah noticed, and wore a cut-away tailcoat over his shirt, which was properly fastened so that it no longer revealed any trace of the smooth skin that had showed beneath it when she had first met him. He had pulled his hair back from his face and tied it in a queue at the nape of his neck, fastening it with a black riband. It threw his bones into high relief, revealing the sharp contours of his face.

"Did you want something?" she enquired.

"Yes. I've come to agree to your suggestion," he said. "I have been thinking it over and it is the most sensible solution to our dilemma. We can split the house in two and need never trouble each other. I have some friends staying with me, but they are agreeable to the arrangement, too."

"Good," said Susannah.

She felt an overwhelming sense of relief. The thought

of spending the next month with the gentleman had been disturbing, but as long as she need never see him, she felt she could endure it.

"As we are going to be fellow inmates, allow me to introduce myself," he said, moving forward. He took Constance's hand and kissed it. "My name is Oliver Bristow."

"Oh, Mr. Bristow! I am Miss Morton. Charmed, I'm sure," said Constance, growing even pinker.

He turned to Susannah, but she did not hold out her hand to him. For some reason she felt wary of letting him kiss it. When he had taken hold of her earlier there had been . . . something. A strange sensation that had made her light-headed, which should have not been pleasurable, but in fact had been exhilarating. Fortunately, it had passed quickly, but she was afraid it might return if he touched her.

"And you are . . . ?" he asked her.

As she did not speak, Constance spoke for her.

"This is Miss Thorpe," Constance said.

"Miss Thorpe," said Oliver, making her a bow.

"It is good of you to introduce yourself," said Susannah.

"Not at all. But I must not take up any more of your time, and I will bid you both good night," he said.

"I thought you said he was not a gentleman?" asked Constance as the door closed behind him. "He seemed very much the gentleman to me."

Susannah did not reply. Something about him disturbed her. She had the feeling there was more to him than was being revealed, and it made her apprehensive. He had been charm itself when speaking to Constance, but earlier there had been something wild about him. Like the sea which could be heard nearby, he seemed to have different moods, and she had the feeling that he was just as dangerous. On the surface he might appear placid when he chose, but there were still rocks beneath the surface, ready to dash the unwary to pieces.

"The kitchens were very well stocked," said Constance, breaking into her thoughts. "I brought some biscuits to go with our tea. Won't you have one?"

"Yes, I will, thank you," said Susannah. She brought her thoughts back to the mundane with relief. It was far easier to think of tea and biscuits than it was to think of Oliver Bristow. "I'm hungry. It seems a long time since we stopped for supper."

After finishing their drink, Susannah said, "I think we should choose our bedchambers. It's already late, and we might have to make up the beds."

Constance agreed, and after taking the tray back to the kitchen and washing the dishes, she rejoined Susannah. There were ominous creaks as they crossed the hall and ascended the stairs, and Susannah was grateful for Constance's company. It would have seemed frightening without her, but as the two of them shared a smile at each new groan of the floorboards, and laughed at the wind moaning along the corridor, it seemed like an adventure.

Once they reached the half-landing they hesitated, then Susannah took the left branch. At the top, she turned to the right and opened the first door. It led into a large room, but seeing a razor and shaving brushes on its washstand, she hastily retreated.

"I think we are in the wrong wing," she said.

She and Constance turned round and went in the opposite direction. Trying another door, Susannah found an empty bedchamber. It was a cramped apartment, and she tried the next. It was much more spacious, but had very little furniture. There was no washstand, and no wardrobe. The next one looked more promising.

As Constance followed her in, she said, "Oh, my!"

It was a huge apartment with a massive four-poster bed in the middle of it. Red velvet curtains hung round the bed, and heavy oak furniture was pushed back against the walls. There was a wardrobe, a chest of drawers, a washstand, a wing chair, a desk and a shield-backed chair, and at the foot of the bed there was a blanket box. Tall windows looked over the open countryside at the back of the house, which was silvered by the moon. "Oh, my," she said again.

"I think this should be your room," said Susannah.

"I shall feel like a queen sleeping here!" said Constance.

"Then I will see you in the morning, Your Majesty," Susannah teased.

Leaving Constance to enjoy the splendours of her new apartment, Susannah examined a further two chambers before choosing one for herself. It was smaller than Constance's room, but it overlooked the sea. Even in the dark the ocean was a magnificent sight, stretching out as far as the eye could see. Susannah had wanted to see it again after spending the early part of her life on the coast, and here it was, a never-ending expanse of water, moving like a thing alive, a giant turning beneath a silver-grey counterpane that sparkled and shimmered in the starlight.

She put her portmanteau by the wing chair then lit the candles on the mantelpiece. There was another candle on the table by the bed. She moved it slightly so that it was not in any danger of setting the bed hangings alight and then lit it, before setting her candelabra on the mantelpiece.

In the dancing light she took in the room where she was to spend the next month. The four-poster looked ancient, but as she tested the mattress, she was pleased to find it was comfortable. Better yet, it was already made up with clean, dry sheets. She should unpack her portmanteau, she thought, but she was too tired. Instead, she simply took out her gowns and hung them in the wardrobe so that the creases could hang out, then left the rest of her scant possessions for the morning.

She was about to draw the curtains when she decided she would leave them open. The sight of the sea soothed her, and she wanted to see it if she woke in the night.

An exciting day, Constance had called it. Yes, it had been exciting, reflected Susannah, but it had also been unsettling. And the most unsettling part of it had been her meeting with Oliver Bristow.

CHAPTER THREE

The next morning the weather was stormy. Drawn by the sight of the turbulent water, Susannah climbed out of bed and went over to the window. The wind was whipping the waves into white peaks. Clouds hung low over the sea, and scudded across the sky. She stayed watching the waves until a draught from the window stirred her nightgown and she shivered. It was time to dress. There was no water in the bowl on the washstand, and she wondered whether she should go down to the kitchen in her wrapper, but the notion that she might bump into Mr. Bristow decided her against it. She would wash later, after breakfast, instead. She was just about to slip her nightgown over her head when there was a knock at the door.

"Who is it?" she called.

"It's Constance. I have brought you some hot water."

"What a blessing!"

Susannah opened the door and saw that Constance was already dressed. She was wearing the same grey gown and mob cap she had worn many times before, yet she was looking younger than usual, and Susannah realized it was because she had lost her harried look. She had always worn it at Mrs. Russell's house, and small wonder. But this morning she was smiling.

"It's a beautiful morning," said Constance, apparently oblivious to the storm. "I will make breakfast as soon as you come downstairs."

Susannah took the jug of hot water gratefully, and was soon splashing it into the bowl. In the clear light of day she could see how fine the porcelain was. It was almost translucent, and was painted with birds and flowers. Next to the dark oak of the washstand it seemed even more delicate, and it was far nicer than anything she had had at Mrs. Russell's house. Having washed, she slipped on her chemise and then tied her quilted petticoat round her waist. She fastened her blue, open skirt on top of it so the petticoat was revealed, then donned the matching bodice. Draping a fichu round her shoulders, she secured it with a brooch and then completed her toilette with a wide blue sash round her waist. It was a pity her shoes were brown, she reflected, but when she inherited her

42

fortune she would have shoes dyed to match every new dress.

She brushed her hair, then pinned it up as best she could, leaving one swathe to drape over her left shoulder. She had not had the inclination to set it in rags the night before, so it was straight, not curled, but at least her hairstyle was a little more fashionable than the one she had been forced to adopt as a governess.

Once ready, she went downstairs. In the daytime, the house seemed less forbidding, and when she entered the sitting-room she found that Constance was already there.

"Oh, good!" said Constance, jumping up. "I will go and make breakfast."

"I didn't bring you here to wait on me," said Susannah. "I might have told Mr. Bristow you were my companion, but that was only to let him know that I wasn't alone. If you hadn't befriended me when I first arrived at the Russells' house, my life would have been very bleak, and I'm glad I've been able to repay you. I don't see you as a servant, Constance. I see you as a friend."

"Thank you, Susannah, you are very kind. But I cannot impose on you for ever." She hesitated, then said, "I was wondering if you might need a housekeeper. I used to keep house for my father before he died and I enjoyed it. Might you consider appointing me?"

Constance had shrunk as a companion, where she had

been constantly belittled and put upon, but she had already regained much of her confidence away from Mrs. Russell, and Susannah thought the idea a splendid one. As a house-keeper, Constance would be the queen of her own domain, and would have a maid to wait on her. Seeing the energy with which she had spoken of the idea, Susannah decided it would be a very good thing for both of them.

"Oh, yes, it will take a weight off my mind," she said gratefully. "Mr. Sinders said it was difficult to engage staff to work here in the summer, and I was wondering how I was going to manage by myself."

"And now I will make breakfast. No, it's no use pro-testing," Constance said gaily. "You can't make breakfast because you don't know where the kitchen is!"

Susannah smiled. "I will have to find out before long, but thank you."

She looked round the room when Constance had gone. It was surprisingly well kept, and with the roaring fire Con-stance had lit, it was very comfortable. The wallpaper was of a faded cream colour, the chairs were upholstered in silk, and the furniture was made of walnut. It was dull with ne-glect, but it would be beautiful when it was polished. Con-stance returned a short while later with a tray of hot rolls and chocolate, and as they ate, they talked over their plans for the morning.

"I am going to attend to the dining-room," said Constance. "We cannot go on balancing plates on our knees in the sitting-room for ever. The dining-room is a fine chamber. The table is dusty and the fire is unlit, but that is easy to alter."

"I'd like to explore the estate, but it's impossible," Susannah said. The wind was howling round the house, and rain spattered against the window. "I think I will explore the house instead."

The two ladies finished their breakfast, and whilst Constance embarked on her mission to make the dining-room habitable, Susannah went upstairs, deciding she would start at the top of the house and work downwards. She wanted to see in what state of repair the house was, so that she would know if any restoration work needed carrying out. She walked along the landing in search of stairs to the attic, and at last found them tucked away in the far corner of the west wing. They were narrow, and made of unpolished wood, but with a carpet they could be made very pleasant.

At the top she came out on to a long landing with windows overlooking the sea. There were two doors along the corridor's length, and one at each end. She decided to start with the nearest door, and found herself in a spacious chamber, with heavy beams supporting a sloping roof. The window on the opposite wall looked north over the countryside. It was covered in cobwebs, but it was a good size, and when cleaned it would make the most of the wonderful view. There were no other houses in sight, and she could see for miles.

She turned her attention inwards. There was an accumulation of broken furniture on the floor, with some mouldy bedding and an old-fashioned chest. Dust covered everything, and swirled in the draught from the open door. Some of the furniture was fit only for throwing away, but there was a fine Louis Seize chair that would be beautiful if it was re-covered, and a long-case clock which was very handsome. Its hands were stuck at half-past eleven, but perhaps it could be repaired. She dismissed the bedding as irreclaimable and then opened the chest. A cloud of dust rose around her, making her sneeze. Inside, there were some old clothes of a kind fashionable thirty years before. She sifted through them, taking out a hooped petticoat, a set of panniers, a long apron and a powdered wig. The clothes made her smile, but there was nothing worth using, so she put everything away and closed the chest again.

She gave one last look around, noting the room's fine dimensions. If Constance wanted, she could have the top floor of one wing entirely to herself. It would provide her with an attractive set of rooms, and plenty of space. She must mention the idea when she went downstairs.

Leaving the room behind, Susannah examined the other rooms one by one, finding most of them empty, until she reached the last room, which was at the end of the corridor. It was smaller than the others, and overlooked the sea. It contained more broken furniture, some old curtains and a pile of old books. The curtains appeared to be in good condition, and were made of a heavy blue silk. Susannah picked them up, sneezing again as the dust stirred, and examined them for holes, but they were sound. Perhaps they would fit the windows in the larger room once they had been cleaned, she reflected. She would see if there was a wash house in the basement, for if there was, she could take everything that needed cleaning and mending and leave it there until she had time to attend to it.

She folded the curtains and set them down on a chipped table. As she did so, she saw a number of items which had been hidden beneath them. There was a storm lantern, which appeared to be in good condition, a walking cane with its top missing, and a globe. She picked up the lantern. Beneath the curtains it had been protected from the dust, and its glass was complete. She decided to take it downstairs with her, thinking it might come in useful. Picking up the curtains and throwing them over her arm, she was about to go downstairs when she caught the sound of a creaking stair. She thought Constance must have come to join her, but it was not Constance who walked into the room a moment later, it was Oliver Bristow.

"Mr. Bristow!" she exclaimed in surprise.

"Miss Thorpe." He smiled charmingly. "I saw you coming up to the attic, and I thought you might need some help. There are some rotting floorboards that are best avoided. They were pointed out to me when I took the house, and I thought I would tell you where they are."

"I see. Thank you. I would rather not fall through the floor! I am just familiarizing myself with the house," she explained.

"So I guessed." He crossed the room and looked out of the window, then looked round the attic. "It's a fine room. Are you thinking of using it when you inherit?"

"Yes. I thought Constance might like one wing of the attic rooms for her own."

He raised his eyebrows. "An entire wing? You must think highly of your companion."

"She won't be my companion for much longer. She is going to be my housekeeper."

"I see."

"It's very difficult to get staff here in the summer, I understand. How have you managed?"

"We brought our own servant, Kelsey, with us," he said, leaning back against the window ledge and putting his hands behind him to protect his leather breeches from the dirt. He stretched his long legs out in front of him and crossed them at the ankles. His pose was careless, but even so, she had the feeling that a whipcord strength lay just beneath the surface, ready to be used if necessary. She felt apprehensive, as though she was in the room with a wild animal that was behaving in a tame and friendly fashion, but which could reveal its predatory nature at any moment. But it would not do to let him see that she was afraid.

"Servant? Only one?" she asked.

"Yes, only one, and he is mainly here for the comfort of our horses. My friends and I prefer to fend for ourselves when we are out of town. Being waited on makes a man soft."

Soft was not a word she would use to describe Oliver Bristow, she thought, as she glanced at the hard ridges of his muscles beneath his tailcoat.

"I have finished my work in the attic," she said. "I was just about to go downstairs."

"Then you must let me carry your things."

"Thank you. I've been sorting through everything that has been abandoned here. Most of it is unusable, but one or two items can be salvaged. The lantern will be useful when I go out into the yard in the mornings, and the curtains will be beautiful once they've been washed."

He looked at the lantern and a strange expression crossed his face, but he said nothing, and they started to go downstairs.

"Have you been at Harstairs House long?" she asked him.

"Almost six months," he replied. "We took the house in June. The lease has nearly run its course."

"It seems a very remote spot to choose. What made you come here?"

"I am thinking of buying an estate here. It made sense to rent one as a base whilst I accustomed myself to the area and saw what was on offer. Besides, it makes a change from the clamour of London."

"You don't like London?" she asked, her eyes lighting up.

"I like it well enough in small doses, but it seems you prefer it to the country?" he said, smiling at her enthusiasm.

"I don't know. I've never been, so I really can't say."

"Never?" he asked, lifting one eyebrow.

"No."

"But you intend to go?" he asked.

"Yes, I do. There is so much I want to do and see. I want to visit the galleries and go to the theatres and the shops. I want to walk in Green Park and ride in Rotten Row, although why it should be called rotten when it is by all accounts very pleasant, I don't know!"

"It's a corruption of *route de roi*, the king's road," he said.

"Ah! Then I will enjoy it all the more."

He smiled, but then his face took on an unreadable expression. "You seem to know a lot about London for someone who's never been," he remarked.

For one unsettling moment she thought he didn't believe her. But why should he not?

"My great aunt told me about it," she explained. "She visited London when she was a girl, and never forgot it. Some of her friends still live there. They used to send her up-to-date fashion journals and tell her all the news, and now that she's dead, some of them still write to me."

Lost in happy memories of her great aunt she forgot to be uncomfortable and, as they descended to the hall, talking of London, she found herself enjoying his company.

Once they reached the bottom of the stairs, a young gentleman emerged into the hall from the direction of the library, followed by an older man.

"You must be Miss Thorpe," said the young man.

"Yes?" said Susannah enquiringly.

"Mr. James Owen," he introduced himself, bowing over her hand.

"I am pleased to meet you," said Susannah.

"And I am Mr. Edward Catling," said the older man, bowing over her hand in his turn.

"My friends are bearing me company in Cornwall," said Oliver. "It would be very dull by myself. Shall we?"

They took their leave of the other gentlemen, and Oliver guided her to the kitchen. It was a homely room with a fire blazing in the hearth. A spitjack was set in front of it and a kettle was hanging over it. A large table, which had been scrubbed until it was almost white, dominated the centre of the room, and a dresser, stocked with plates, goblets, pans and dishes, was pushed back against the far wall. He deposited the curtains on a wooden chair and put the lantern on the mantelpiece.

"I will leave you now," he said, as Constance entered the room carrying an empty coal scuttle. "I'm sure you have plenty to do."

"I must say, I think we have been fortunate to have such a charming tenant," said Constance, as the door closed behind him. "And so attentive. He seems very taken with you, Susannah."

"He was kind enough to warn me of some rotting floorboards in the attic, and offered to carry some things downstairs for me, that's all," said Susannah, feeling uncomfortable.

"I'm sure you don't need to explain his presence to me," said Constance gaily, filling the scuttle from a large bucket of coal next to the fire.

I wasn't explaining, Susannah was about to say, when she decided it was better to leave the subject alone, for she had just realized that although Mr. Bristow had said he joined her to warn her about rotting floorboards, he had not actually pointed any out to her.

"I thought it would be a good idea to put all the linen that needs mending or cleaning in the wash house, if there is such a thing," said Susannah, changing the subject. "Then it is all in one place when we have time to attend to it."

"Oh, yes, there's a very good wash house, although it's not very well situated. It's through the door over there," said Constance.

Susannah's eyes followed her gaze. They came to rest on one of the doors leading from the far side of the kitchen, next to the dresser. Susannah went through it and found herself in a large room with a huge fireplace. A copper was placed over it, and an airing rack hung from the ceiling. A large table was pushed back against one wall.

"There's no door to the yard, so we will have to bring the water through the kitchen from the well," said Constance, following her. "But there is plenty of room for drying things, as well as washing them, and the airing rack will be very useful."

"Good. Then we will store things here until I can see about hiring some more servants."

"Yes, we will need them. There is a lot to be done," said Constance, "but I have no doubt there'll be girls in the village who will be glad of the work."

Susannah piled the curtains on the long table, then hesitated.

"I'm not being precipitate, am I? I haven't inherited the house yet, but I have already started to organize it. Perhaps I should wait?"

"No, I don't think so," said Constance. "You are not doing anything that can't be undone if, by any chance, you don't inherit. But why shouldn't you? The house doesn't seem to be haunted, and even if we wake to find a spectre rattling its chains, I am sure we are its equal!"

Susannah smiled. "I never knew you were so brave," she said.

Constance smiled back. "Neither did I. But it is surprising what a difference a little happiness makes! Besides, the sooner we sort out the house, the better."

"How are you faring with the dining-room?" asked Susannah, as Constance picked up the filled coal scuttle and they went upstairs again.

"I have dusted it and lit the fire. It should soon flare up and make a nice, bright blaze."

They parted in the hall, Constance returning to the dining-room to replace the coal scuttle and polish the table, and Susannah going into the sitting-room to write a letter to Mrs. Wise. Mrs. Wise was one of her great aunt's friends, and she had always taken a kindly interest in Susannah. It was through Mrs. Wise's kind offices that Susannah had found her first position, which had been as a companion to a cheerful old lady by the name of Mrs. Ormond. Susannah had enjoyed herself, until Mrs. Ormond had emigrated to be with her son and she had had to take a post as a governess, but now she wanted to let Mrs. Wise know of her good fortune. She took up a quill and paper, and she began to write.

My dear Mrs. Wise.

The time passed swiftly, as she had a great deal of news to impart. Once she had finished her letter, she folded it and sealed it with wax, then put it in her pocket, ready to give to the boy who brought the milk the following morning.

As she thought of going out to meet him at daybreak, she remembered the lantern she had found, and wondered for a moment why it had been left in the attic. Everything else had been dirty, or in a poor state of repair, but the lamp had been almost new. She was just pondering the puzzle when Constance came back into the room.

"Well, that is done. We should be able to have lunch in there today. I have just met the other two gentlemen who are sharing the house with us—Mr. Bristow's friends," she continued. "They were about to go out riding. Such pleasant gentlemen. They told me we must not hesitate to ask for assistance if we need any help chopping wood or carrying coal. So thoughtful."

"Yes, I met them earlier," remarked Susannah.

"It makes such a difference to have gentlemen about the house. I feel so much safer with them here."

Susannah did not reply to this remark. The one thing she never felt with Mr. Bristow was safe. But since she could hardly tell Constance that his air of power unsettled her, she turned the subject by asking what they should have for lunch.

~ ~ ~

The three gentlemen crossed the hall and went out of the front door, heading towards the coast.

"I think this was a mistake," said Edward darkly. "The ladies have only been in the house a few hours, and already we've run across them twice. It's going to be impossible keeping them away from us."

"What harm can it do if they see us in the hall occasionally?" asked James nonchalantly. "We make a little conversation, offer them our help, and they go on their way—as we go on ours."

"And what were you doing with the lantern?" said Edward, turning to look at Oliver, who was striding along beside him. "Why were you carrying it down from the attic?"

"Miss Thorpe found it there. Don't worry," he said, seeing Edward's expression. "She didn't know what it was for. She thought it was part of the ordinary rubbish that had been deposited there. Deeming it useful, she decided to take it down to the kitchen."

"Can women never leave anything alone?" asked Edward, in exasperation. "What was she doing in the attic anyway?"

"Seeing how much work it would take to make it habitable. She is thinking of using it as servants' quarters."

"Or so she says. But whatever her reasons for being there, she has taken the lantern, and now we will have to find another one to signal with."

"A small problem," said Oliver.

"She's a menace. I wish she had never come to the house."

"Oliver doesn't think so," said James with a wicked smile, as they walked across the cliffs.

Edward looked at him sharply. "What do you mean?"

James glanced at Oliver. "Oliver's on the hunt."

"On the hunt?" enquired Edward with a frown.

"He's stalking Miss Thorpe!"

"What's this?" demanded Edward. "I hope you haven't been doing anything foolish, Oliver?"

"Of course not," said Oliver, as he strode across the cliffs with his black hair rippling in the breeze. "It's nothing."

"So," continued James, "how do you think you are getting on? Is she in love with you yet? Has she fallen under your spell? Has she been conquered by your charm?"

Oliver looked at him with mild amusement. "You seem sure I've set out to conquer her, but perhaps I've no fancy for her."

"That doesn't usually stop you, and in this case I'm certain it won't."

"Meaning?"

"Meaning that as soon as she said she wouldn't marry you if her life depended on it, her fate was sealed!"

"What folly is this?" asked Edward sharply. "You haven't asked her to marry you?"

"Of course not. What do you take me for?"

"Then why . . . ?"

"The companion thought they'd make a handsome couple," said James with a grin. "Oliver overheard them talking when he went to tell them we'd decided to share the house. But little Miss Hard-to-please said she wouldn't marry him to save her life—which, to Oliver, is tantamount to slapping his face with a glove. It's a challenge he can't resist."

Oliver gave a wolfish smile.

"No, you can't do it," said Edward, stopping to look at him angrily. "I forbid it."

Oliver returned his gaze. He spoke softly, but there was a glitter in his eyes. "I will allow no man to forbid me anything. Not even you."

"Think about what you're doing, for God's sake!" exclaimed Edward. "It's not only stupid to get involved with her, it's cruel. The girl's had no experience of life. She's spent most of it in the schoolroom. She's no match for a man like you."

"You make too much of things," said Oliver, with a shrug of his massive shoulders. "It's nothing important, just a little harmless flirtation, that's all."

"For you maybe, but for her?"

"Don't worry, I know when to stop. The fair sex may look delicate on the outside, but on the inside they are quite the reverse. It won't do her any lasting harm," he said. "It will simply give her an autumn to remember."

"If she finds out what we're doing here, it could give us an autumn to remember," growled Edward.

"She won't," replied Oliver curtly.

"She had better not. You really mean to go through with this"—he gestured with his hands—"this foolery?"

Oliver nodded. "I rather think I do."

"I don't know what happened to you in France, Oliver," said Edward in disgust, "but it can't have been anything good."

"Nothing that happens in France is good any more," said James, sobering suddenly. "It is all terrible."

"This is more than the general horror. It's personal, something that happened before the troubles took a hold," said Edward, looking at Oliver intently.

"What happened to me in France is my own business," said Oliver.

James looked from one to the other of them.

"What was it?" asked James curiously. "What did happen, Oliver?"

Oliver's face grew dark. "Be thankful you don't know."

CHAPTER FOUR

Susannah was looking forward to sending her letter to Mrs. Wise and rose early the following morning. She went down to the kitchen, where she eagerly awaited the arrival of the boy who delivered the milk. She heard footsteps coming across the yard just as dawn was breaking, and the sound of a breathy noise as someone whistled a popular ditty. Opening the door, she went out into the yard and saw a boy of about twelve years old coming towards her. His coat was too big for him and his baggy trousers were held up by a piece of string. He had red hair and freckles, and both were set off by a cheeky grin.

"Mornin', miss," he said, as he set down a pitcher of milk and a box of eggs. "It be a proper 'un this mornin' and no mistake." He looked up at the sky as he spoke, leading Susannah to guess that he was talking about the weather.

"Yes, it's a lovely day," she agreed. "I have a letter for you to take for me, please. Mr. Sinders said he had made arrangements for my letters to be delivered."

"Ais, miss, I'll see to it," said the boy, taking it from her and putting it in his coat pocket.

"I am expecting a reply. Will you be able to bring it to me?"

"Ais, miss, don't you worry, miss, I'll see to it fer 'ee," he said cheerfully.

"Do you call at the house every day?" she asked, wondering when she could expect a reply to her letter.

"Ais, miss, every day 'cept Christmas day. Milk and eggs each mornin'. Fish on Fridays, meat on Mondays and Thursdays, and cheese whenever you asks fer it."

"We have enough for the moment, thank you, but we will need some more on Saturday."

"Ais, miss. A nice piece o' ripe cheese on Saturday. Be you settlin' in, miss?" he asked conversationally.

"Yes, thank you," she said.

He looked up at the house.

"A rare big 'ouse is 'arstairs, miss."

"Yes," she said with a sigh, thinking of all the rooms that needed cleaning. It would take her and Constance months to see to it.

"It'll take a deal o' work keepin' it in good order," he said.

"You seem to have read my mind," she remarked.

"I got sisters, miss, two of 'em, both 'ardworking," he said suggestively.

She was beginning to realize there was a point to his conversation and she became more interested.

"Do you mean you think they would like to come here and work as maids?" she asked with interest.

"Don't know about maids, miss, but rare good at cleaning they be."

"Thank you . . . I don't know your name?" she said.

"Jim, miss."

"Well, then, thank you, Jim. I think that's an excellent idea—a rare idea," she said with a smile, as she started to understand his way of speaking. "Can you ask them to call on me? I will not inherit the house until next month, and then I daresay there will be formalities to be attended to, but shall we say on 15th December?"

"When be that, miss?"

"In a few weeks' time," she said. "I will remind you on the day before I'd like them to call."

"Ais, miss."

Susannah was about to go back inside when she noticed that he was lingering.

"Is there anything else, Jim?"

"Jus' lookin' at your kitchen garden, miss. A regular mess, it do be. Seems a shame to waste it like that," he said.

Susannah followed his gaze to a patch of earth which must have once been a thriving garden. It contained a few forlorn wilted leaves, a mass of weeds, and earth that had not seen a shovel or a fork in months.

"Yes, I must see to it. Unfortunately, I'm not much of a gardener," said Susannah ruefully.

"Not much work 'ereabouts in the winter," said Jim. "I reckon someone'd be glad to look a'ter it for 'ee."

"You don't know of anyone who might do it, I suppose?" asked Susannah.

"My father be good with a garden, miss," he said.

"Then he must come to see me when your sisters come," she said with a smile.

"Ais, I reckon so," said Jim. Still Jim lingered. "I be good with 'orses, miss," he volunteered.

"It seems I am going to have your whole family working for me!" she said.

"No, miss," he said, shaking his head. "My brothers, they do work down the mine. Copper miners they be. You won't catch 'em working 'ere, but spending all day in the dark baint for me. A stablehand, then groom, then coachman, that's the job for me," he said with a cheeky grin.

"Be off with you!" said Susannah, laughing. "You'll have

to muck out many a stable before you drive a coach! But bring your father and sisters with you in December, and we will see."

"Ais, miss."

He touched his forehead in a sign of respect and then, bidding her a good morning, he walked back the way he had come, his cheery whistle fading into the early morning stillness.

Susannah went back into the kitchen, still smiling, and found Constance setting the kettle on a trivet over the fire.

"You look pleased," said Constance, straightening up.

"I am pleased. I have just been offered the services of half of Jim's family! Jim is the boy who brings the milk," she explained. "It seems as though we will have two maids, a gardener and a stable-boy before we've been here very much longer."

"Well!" said Constance in surprise, as she set two dishes on a tray. "That does sound promising. Unless . . ."

"Yes?" said Susannah.

"I only hope that he and his family are not dishonest."

"He seemed a nice enough boy, but I will ask for references, and you can interview them before they start work," said Susannah.

"Perhaps it would also be wise to ask Mr. Sinders to make sure there is nothing known against them in the neighbourhood. We don't want to wake up one morning and find all the silver missing."

"A good idea. But I hope they are honest. Two hard-working girls would be a great help, and make our lives a lot easier. There is already a large pile in the wash house, and it will be bigger before we have finished."

"If we're to have help, I'll start looking through some of the spare bedrooms this morning and check the linen," said Constance. "We might as well make a clean sweep of it whilst we're about it."

"I think I'll explore the estate. It's a beautiful morning, and I want to make the most of the weather. Who knows when the next fine day might come along?"

She helped Constance prepare the breakfast, and after the two of them had eaten their fill, Susannah repaired to her bedroom. How nice it would be to have a new cloak, one that was not frayed, and a new pair of half boots that were not scuffed and worn! she thought as she dressed herself for the outdoors. She pinned her tall hat to her head, tying it beneath her chin with a ribbon, then fastened her cloak round her shoulders and pulled on her gloves. Going down-stairs she went out into the garden and felt she was ready to brave the bright but blustery day. The wind whipped at the hem of her cloak, but it was playful rather than brutal, and she set off at a vigorous pace. She walked round the house, passing an overgrown drive at the back that led westward to the stables, but she ignored it. She struck out towards the coast. The grass was wet, and she was glad of her sturdy half boots. They would let the water in eventually, but for a short time at least they would keep her feet dry.

She crossed the lawn, and soon found herself on the coarser grass of the cliff tops. It was brown in patches, despite the recent rain, and was littered with rocks and boulders. Beyond it lay the sea.

Holding her hat on with her hand, she leant into the wind. It stung her cheeks, but it was exhilarating. At last she stood on the edge of the cliff and looked out over the water. It was calm, with only a gentle swell, and it was as blue as the sky, topped with occasional white peaks. As long as she looked outwards she did not realize how high up she was, but when her eyes dropped, she realized that the cliff towered over the boulders below. The spray was beating against the foot of the cliffs beneath her, sending spume flying into the air. But further round the coast, the scene was more peaceful, and the sea washed into a cove. It was small but sandy and it appeared to be sheltered, and she had a longing to walk on the sand. She let her eyes wander along the cliff face. Although it was steep it was not sheer, and she thought it possible that there might be a path leading downwards at some point. She could not see one, but turning left, she followed the cliff as it undulated with the coast.

Going on a little further, she found what she had been

seeking, a path cutting its way backwards and forwards across the cliff to the beach below. Her half boots made light work of the path, but she had to use her hands to help her in one or two places where the slope was steep, and she was forced to scramble down the last twenty feet. She brushed her hands against each other, knocking the soil and sand from her kid gloves, then walked to the water's edge. The sand was soft but firm beneath her feet.

The tide was so low she thought she would be able to walk round the coast. Deciding to risk the slippery rocks to her left, she soon traversed them, and turning a corner she found herself in another cove. She walked on, rounding the rocks into the next cove. It was even smaller than the last one, but it had a natural jetty made out of boulders washed up by the tide. Next to the jetty was a rowing boat, fastened to a pole sticking out of the water. It seemed to be in a good state of repair. There were two seats running across it, and the oars were neatly tucked away, but the rowlocks were missing. They had evidently been taken away by the prudent owner so that the boat could not be stolen.

Her mind went back to her childhood, when her father had kept a boat and had rowed her out to sea on many occasions. They had been happy times. As she had grown older, he had taught her how to row, and though small and not very strong, she had managed to acquire the rhythm. She wondered if she still remembered how to do it. She would have to ask the locals about the tides and currents, and then she would take up rowing again, she decided. There was nothing pleasanter on a summer's day than sculling across the waves with the sun on her face and the sound of the gulls in her ears.

She began to grow cold. She had been standing for some time, and the wind was growing stronger. Deciding to return to the house, she retraced her steps until she reached the cliff path. She slipped once going up, but her worn boots helped her regain her footing and she was soon at the top. With a last look at the ocean she turned inland, crossing the cliffs and walking back to the house. As she approached the garden, she saw a figure she recognized coming from the stable-yard. It was Oliver Bristow. She had an unaccountable desire to turn aside, but telling herself not to be so foolish she carried on her way. What did it matter if she met Mr. Bristow?

"Good morning," said Oliver with a bow, as the two of them converged. "Have you been exploring?"

"Yes. It was such a beautiful morning I couldn't bear to be inside."

"Did you go far?" he asked, falling into step beside her as she carried on her way back to the house.

"Down to the beach," she said. "There's a path down the side of the cliff, leading into the coves. They will be lovely in the summer time."

"I would advise you not to go there too often," he said. "The sea looks pretty, but it wouldn't do to underestimate it. It can be deadly."

He stopped walking and stood looking back at the water.

"How so?"

"The tide comes in very rapidly." He turned back to look at her. "It would be better if you stayed in the gardens around the house."

"What? Never go down to the beach? It's one of the best parts of inheriting Harstairs House!" she protested. "I mean to hold picnics there in the summer."

"In the summer, yes, but in the winter the coast is treacherous, and only one of the coves has access to a path. The others are completely submerged at high tide."

"But there would be time to get back to the path?" she enquired.

"Not always, no. If you were in the next cove, then perhaps, but the water comes in very quickly and not even that would always be possible. A slip on the rocks and a minute lost can make the difference between life and death."

"Is the tide really so quick?" she asked in surprise.

"It is. Unwary people are often cut off, and several people have been swept away since we've been here. Their bodies were not found for weeks, and when they were, they were so badly eroded by the tide they were unrecognizable."

"You are trying to frighten me," she said.

"To warn you," he replied.

His whole attitude was a warning. Although he was standing casually, she felt an air of tension coming from him, and she noticed that his muscles were bunched beneath his breeches and coat.

"Very well," she said hesitantly. "I will take care."

He nodded. "I am not trying to spoil your pleasure in your inheritance, but it's as well to know about these things."

"Do you have a table of the tides?" she asked. "If there are other fine days I would like to go down to the sea again, even if I stay in the cove at the bottom of the path, and it should be safe enough at low tide," she said.

"No, I'm afraid I don't."

He spoke abruptly, and Susannah wondered for a moment whether he was being honest with her. But why should he lie about such a thing? Besides, there was no reason why he should know about the tides. She would have to ask Jim.

"It can't be so dangerous," said Susannah musingly, as she quickened her step to keep up with him. "I found a boat in one of the coves, so Mr. Harstairs must have gone out from time to time. I must try and find the rowlocks. They had been taken away, but they must be stored somewhere in the house. I didn't find them in the attic, but it is not surprising as they would be in constant use over the summer months. Perhaps they are in the kitchen."

"No, they are not," he said, as they reached the house and went inside. "The boat doesn't belong to Harstairs House: it belongs to me. I brought it here hoping to use it, but the currents are so strong that I only took it out once. Fortunately, Edward was with me, and it was all we could do to get back to shore safely. Even with both of us rowing, the tide almost carried us out to sea. Believe me, it is better if you keep away." His eyes looked down into her own. "If you want to go down to the shore then I can't stop you, but please, take care. I would not like any harm to come to you."

He took her hand as he said it, and she felt her heart skip a beat. The skin on the palm of her hand grew hot where he touched it even through her glove, and as he kissed her hand she felt suddenly restless. Her eyes were drawn to his and what she saw there made her eyelids droop. But just before her eyes closed, she caught sight of his mouth, and saw with a jolt that his smile had changed. It looked almost cruel. Shaken, she opened her eyes wide, but the cruel look had gone, and she thought she must have imagined it.

"It's a wild country," he said, as he dropped her hand. "You are not used to it, but you will become so. Don't underestimate the dangers all around you."

Then making her a low bow, he headed for the back of the house, leaving her alone in the hall.

Dangers, she thought, as she returned to her room to remove her outdoor things. Perhaps the sea was dangerous, but she had the alarming feeling that Oliver Bristow was even more dangerous. He seemed to unsettle her whenever he was near, and she was not sure how he managed to do so. On the surface he was everything that was polite and charming, but underneath the surface something wilder lurked. Even more alarming, it called to something wild in herself that she had never even known existed before coming to Harstairs House.

The discomfort of her wet feet brought her back to her surroundings, and a glance downwards showed her that her boots were soiled with sand. Inside them she could feel her stockings squelching. Slipping her cloak from her shoulders and removing her hat, she sat down on the bed, and changed her boots and stockings. But the memory of Oliver's kiss lingered as she descended the stairs and joined Constance in the sitting-room, and she found she could almost still feel it on her hand.

It was warm in the sitting-room. The fire was blazing in the inglenook, and Constance was sitting and darning a sheet. It was a homely scene, and yet even this could not completely rid Susannah of the unsettling feelings she had experienced when she had been with Oliver.

"Did you enjoy your walk?" asked Constance, looking up as Susannah entered the room.

"I did," said Susannah, pulling her thoughts away from Oliver with difficulty. "You must come with me the next time I go. The estate is beautiful, in a vigorous way, and the weather was exhilarating. When the wind blows in from the sea, the tang of salt is enlivening," she said, as she tasted it on her lips.

"Did you manage to go down to the shore?" asked Constance.

"Yes, there's a path cut into the face of the cliff, and I managed to explore several coves before turning back. It was cold, but pleasant when the sun came out, and it will be wonderful in the summer."

Going over to the fireplace, Susannah warmed her hands at the blaze. It reminded her of a moment, two days ago, when she had longed to warm her hands in Mrs. Russell's drawing-room and had not dared to do so.

"I can't believe it's only forty-eight hours since we were shivering at Mrs. Russell's," she said. "Such a lot has happened since then that it feels more like a week."

"It certainly does," said Constance, "although a very enjoyable week. I was luckier than you at the Russells' house, I believe, for I spent most of my time in the drawing-room with Mrs. Russell, and at least I was warm."

"I think I was the lucky one," returned Susannah. "I

might not have had a fire, but at least I didn't have to listen to Mrs. Russell's constant complaining!"

"No. It was very wearing," agreed Constance, resting her darning in her lap. "I feel so much better away from her. I have far more energy, and now tomorrow seems something to be looked forward to, instead of something to be dreaded." She picked up her darning again. "Was that Mr. Bristow I saw you with?" she asked nonchalantly, as she set another neat stitch. "I was in the kitchen, and I happened to look out of the window. I thought I saw you with a gentleman."

"Yes. I met him returning to the house."

Constance said nothing, but a smile crossed her face.

"I hope you are not going to make anything of it," said Susannah uncomfortably. "It was a coincidence, and nothing more."

"As it was a coincidence he happened to meet you in the attic?" asked Constance innocently.

Susannah was about to say, Yes, when she realized that she did seem to be seeing a lot of Mr. Bristow.

"He's a very handsome gentleman," said Constance.

"Perhaps," said Susannah, tracing the sharp cheekbones and determined chin in her mind's eye.

"I believe he admires you," she said.

"Nonsense," said Susannah, rubbing her hands together and walking away from the fire. "It is just that two people living under the same roof for any length of time will naturally run across each other, that's all."

"I think it is more than that," said Constance.

"Then perhaps it is my fortune he admires," said Susannah lightly.

"I don't believe he knows anything about it. He knows you are to inherit Harstairs House, of course, but nothing else."

"He is looking for a house in this neighbourhood," Susannah reminded her.

"But he cannot like Harstairs House or he would have tried to buy it before now."

"I am very grateful for your concern, but I don't think you need to ask Mr. Bristow about his intentions towards me just yet!" Susannah teased her.

"No, not just yet," said Constance placidly.

The thought of Oliver deliberately seeking her out was so unsettling that Susannah picked up a piece of paper from one of the console tables, wanting to give a new direction to the conversation.

Sofa, it said. *Two wing chairs, one in need of repair. Oak console table with chipped leg* . . .

"What's this?" she asked Constance with interest.

"I have started making an inventory," Constance said. "The idea came to me whilst I was lighting the fire in the dining-room. I noticed the mantelpiece was damaged—it has a piece missing from the side—and I decided to make a note of everything that needed mending in the room."

"What a good idea," said Susannah thoughtfully.

"I mean to make one for every room of the house."

The awkward moment had passed. Oliver Bristow was no longer spoken of, but Susannah could not help thinking that Constance was right. She did seem to be seeing a lot of Mr. Bristow, which led her to wonder if it was accidental or if it was intentional. And if it was intentional, was it because he admired her, as Constance suspected? Or was it for some other reason?

She remembered his first words to her. They had seemed strange at the time, and seemed even stranger now. *Burglar, vagrant—or spy?*

Did he believe that she was spying on him? And if so, why?

CHAPTER FIVE

Susannah and Constance were determined to put their time at Harstairs House to good use, and over the next few days they began to sort through the spare bedrooms in the west wing. Each bed had been made up, and they stripped off the linen to see if it contained any holes. They examined counterpanes, checked mattresses and studied patchwork quilts. They found the linen closet and sorted through everything inside it, deciding what was good enough to use, what should be mended, and what should be thrown away. Bit by bit, the pile in the wash house grew.

"I had a dreadful dream last night," said Susannah, passing a hand over her forehead as she took a rest. "I dreamt that Mr. Sinders' visit had been a mistake, and that I was not to inherit the house at all. The new owner was very annoyed that I had stripped the beds and brought things down from the attic. To make matters worse, the new owner was Mrs. Russell! After making me put everything back again, she sent me up to the nursery, where I found the children intent on murdering each other. Then they all turned into little white ghosts, and I thought, So the house is haunted after all!"

"My dreams have been no better. Last night I dreamt the king and queen came to visit, and I had to give them my room as none of the others were aired. 'I shall feel like a queen in here,' the Queen said as she sat down at my dressing-table! I was hurrying downstairs to see to their supper when I remembered that the bed wasn't made up, and I woke up to find myself plumping the bolster!"

"That's what comes of having cheese for supper!" laughed Susannah.

She looked out of the window as a gleam of sunshine broke through the clouds.

"I need a respite," she said. "The weather seems to be brightening. I think I will make the most of the sunshine by exploring some more of the estate. Will you come with me?"

"No, thank you. I want to finish what I'm doing here. Once I've sorted things out to my satisfaction, the dreams will stop. It is only because I have too much still to do that they are plaguing me—although I think I will have nothing but a dry biscuit for supper tonight, all the same!"

"I saw some stables at the back of the house when I went down to the coast," said Susannah. "I think I will examine them and see if they are sound. If Jim is keen to be a stable-boy, I will have to have a stable to put him in! That reminds me, I must write to Mr. Sinders and find out what he knows about the boy. I will do it this morning, before I go out."

"Is it wise to give the letter to Jim?" asked Constance. "It will be asking for details about him and his family."

"I don't suppose he can read," said Susannah. "Besides, I have no one else to give it to."

"I thought Mr. Bristow might take it into the village for you," said Constance carelessly.

"I would rather not bother him with it," said Susannah firmly.

She left Constance to her work and went into the sitting-room. Taking up her quill, she wrote to Mr. Sinders and asked him for any information he might have about Jim and his family. Then, putting it behind a candlestick on the mantelpiece, she prepared to go out.

Having donned her outdoor clothes she stepped outside, to the raucous cry of the gulls. The weather was bright, and as she felt the sun on her face she found she was looking forward to further exploring. The estate had much more to offer than the shoreline, and she wanted to see how far the cliffs stretched before she came to a fence.

She followed the path round the house, noting the weeds growing through it, and thinking that there would be plenty of work for Jim's father to do, as well as tending the kitchen garden. Perhaps she might even be able to lure some of Jim's brothers away from the copper mines if she paid them well enough. She soon came to the back of the house, where she followed the narrow drive that led to the stables. As she approached them she saw that the stable block was a ramshackle affair. The end stall had collapsed, but as she walked into the yard she was pleased to see that the other stalls appeared to be sound. The yard itself was large and overgrown, but the horse trough at its centre was clean and it was filled with fresh water.

She heard the sound of the horses whickering and snuffling and went over to the stalls. The middle four were occupied. In the first one there was a black stallion with a star on his forehead. In the next two stalls were greys, and a chestnut was in the fourth. He was a beautiful animal with a glossy coat and a thick mane. He nuzzled Susannah's hand as she lifted it to stroke his nose. She had brought nothing for him, but knew she must remember something the next time she came.

She heard footsteps behind her, and turning round she saw Oliver coming towards her. "Miss Thorpe," he said.

"Mr. Bristow."

"What brings you to the stables?" he asked as he joined her.

He was dressed casually, she noticed, as he had been the first time she had seen him. His leather breeches were designed for comfort and practicality, and his boots had seen hard wear. His coat was new but its cut was loose, rather than the tight cut favoured by the gentlemen who spent their lives gaming and drinking in fashionable clubs.

"I wanted to see if they were in need of repair, or if they were fit for use. Do any of the horses belong to the house, or do they all belong to you and your friends?" she continued. "I would like to explore the estate, and it would be easier to do so on horseback than on foot."

"They belong to us. You would be welcome to ride one, but they are not suitable for ladies," he said.

"I think I could ride the chestnut," she replied, looking at the splendid beast appraisingly as she continued to stroke his nose.

"He's too large for you."

"I believe I could manage him."

There was a patronizing glint in his eyes, and it was clear he did not share her belief. Instead of saying so, however, he said, "Unfortunately there are no side saddles in the stables, so I'm afraid you will be disappointed."

She didn't take kindly to being patronized, and replied coolly, "If I have to, I can ride with a man's saddle. My father was an artist, and a very unconventional man. He raised me to spend most of my time out of doors. He had a chestnut similar to this one, and he taught me to ride it. It was smaller, it is true, but then, at the time, so was I."

"But with a man's saddle?" he asked.

"My father knew nothing about a girl's needs. I doubt if he knew what a lady's saddle was."

"Then perhaps you will join me for a ride?"

"By all means," she said.

He saddled his stallion, and then saddled the chestnut. Standing side by side in the yard, the horses made a splendid sight. It was a long time since Susannah had been riding, and she was looking forward to it.

"Where's the mounting block?" she asked, looking round for it.

"There isn't one."

There was still a mocking note in his voice, and she knew he was expecting her to use the lack of a block as an excuse not to ride.

"Then perhaps you would help me up," she said.

He gave a slight shrug, then made a step out of his hand. Thanking the full skirt of her gown and her lack of a corset for giving her unrestricted movement, Susannah put her foot in his hands. She noticed as she did so how large they were, and how fine and tapering his fingers. Then she turned her attention back to her horse. She pushed against his hands and threw herself into the saddle. As she arranged her skirt around her, she was rewarded by the look of surprise and then reluctant admiration in his eyes . . . and then she flushed as his gaze dropped to her ankles. They were no longer covered by her skirt, and were displayed to advantage as she put her foot in the stirrup. Reminding herself that they were encased in half boots, and telling herself not to be so missish, she ignored his glance and turned the chestnut towards the drive.

It felt strange to be in the saddle again, particularly on a horse she did not know, but after a few minutes she began to feel at ease, and by the time they left the yard she was beginning to enjoy herself.

They rode in silence to begin with, but as they reached the edge of the cliff and then turned along it, he said, "I'm impressed."

He spoke lightly, but there was real appreciation of the way she handled the horse beneath his bantering tone.

"He's a beautiful horse, and very well mannered," she said, as she enjoyed his smooth, easy paces. "Is he yours?"

"No. He belongs to Edward."

A feeling of guilt assailed her. She had been so taken up with the idea of riding that she had not thought about the fact she was riding someone else's horse without a by your leave. "I should have asked for his permission before I rode him."

"As you are allowing all three of us to remain at Harstairs House until our lease expires, I think you may safely assume the answer would have been yes," he said, with a quirk at the corner of his mouth.

"I don't remember *allowing* you to stay at Harstairs House," she said teasingly. "I rather think you refused to leave!"

He laughed. "That's true." He turned to look at her. "Do you mind?"

The words were light, but somehow the atmosphere had changed, and instead of seeming like a polite enquiry, the question seemed personal.

"I . . . no, I don't believe I do."

Their eyes met, and she bit her lip. She felt as though she had given too much away, although why that should be when the conversation was a mere commonplace she did not know. She felt she must lighten the conversation, however, and said, "It's always useful to have a gentleman with a pistol in the house in case of ghosts! You do have a pistol?" she asked.

His eyes flashed. "I never go anywhere without one."

"You know, of course, that Harstairs House is meant to be haunted?" she asked. "You have been here longer than I. Have you seen anything untoward?"

"Well, of course, there is the headless horseman in the stable-yard and the white woman wringing her hands in the drawing-room, but apart from that—no, I don't believe I have."

"Have you really . . . ?" she began, when she saw that he was teasing her.

She didn't know how it was, but she found him very easy to speak to. She had always found conversations with gentlemen difficult in the past. She had met a few when living with her great aunt—dear Great Aunt Caroline had felt she should marry, and had frightened all the gentlemen in the village by asking them to supper as soon as she had turned eighteen—but she had had to make an effort to find things to talk about, and had kept a ready fund of questions in her mind to ask. "Gentlemen always like talking about themselves," her aunt had advised her, so she had enquired about their horses, their carriages and their business interests, but the conversation had fallen flat as soon as the questions had been answered. Then, after uncomfortable silences, they had complimented her on her sewing, examples of which could be found all round Aunt Caroline's house, and she had thanked them, and once again silence had reigned. With Oliver, however, without her even thinking about it, the conversation flowed.

"You say your father was an artist. What kind?"

"He was a painter. That's why he wanted to live by the sea. He painted seascapes."

"Was he good?"

"Yes, very good, or at least I thought he was, but his paintings were too wild for most people's tastes. Instead of showing the sea as a placid sheet of water with prosperous boats dotted on its surface and wealthy patrons looking on complacently, he painted storms. He painted in a small hut on the edge of the cliff, with large windows in the wall and ceiling to let in the light. When the weather was violent, he would go to his hut and paint until both he and the storm had exhausted themselves."

"And what did your mother think of him shutting himself away?" he asked. "Ladies are often nervous in storms. Did she not want your father with her?"

She spoke quietly. "My mother died when I was born."

He gave her a sideways glance.

"I'm sorry," he said. "I, too, lost my mother when I was young. She died shortly after my brother was born."

For a moment it was as though there was a connection between them. As they rode to the edge of the cliff and then followed the path along it, she found herself telling him all about her childhood with her father and the many simple pleasures they had enjoyed. Instead of being horrified at her tales of scrambling over cliffs and learning to swim, he had been amused, and she went on to tell him about her father's death. It was something she had not spoken of, not even to Great Aunt Caroline, and she wondered why she had told him so much. But there was something about him that made it easy for her to confide in him.

In return he told her about his mother, his father and his brother, who was studying for the bar, and his Northumberland estate.

The ride was very pleasant. To her right, the sea was blue under the blue sky, and if not for the intense cold it could almost have been July. Here and there, white crests topped the waves. The coastline was an uneven shape, with the cliffs weaving in and out of the water. Sometimes coves of soft sand separated the feet of the cliffs from the water, and sometimes the sea came right up to their base.

"Have you ever been to the boundaries of the estate?" she asked.

"No, I don't believe I have."

"I was hoping to find them."

"I think you would need all day. The estate is massive. Harstairs was a wealthy man and sank much of his fortune into land."

"Did you know him?" she asked.

There was a slight hesitation before he said, "No. But I knew of him. He was well known in these parts."

"Then you didn't know anything about him before you leased the house?"

Again there was a slight hesitation before he said, "No."

"It seems strange he bought this house, only to lease it out," she mused.

"He found Cornwall romantic in the summer, when he bought the house, but when the winter set in he felt isolated and went back to London."

It was plausible, and yet Susannah felt it wasn't quite the truth. For all his charm, there were depths to Oliver that she had not yet plumbed, and she found herself intrigued.

"Do you know how he made his fortune?" she asked.

"No, only that he made it abroad. He was a businessman, and he also speculated."

"Yes, that is what Mr. Sinders told me." She looked across the cliff tops. "If he was a businessman, I'm surprised he didn't open a mine when he came here. One of Great Aunt Caroline's friends married a Cornishman, and he made a fortune from copper."

"He was old by the time he came here. He carried on with the businesses he had already established, but his days of starting new ventures were over."

Susannah looked around her. Over they might have been, but he had still bought wisely with Harstairs House, with its beautiful location and its miles of seafront. Or at least, possibly miles. She was just about to ask whether there was a plan of the house in the library, thinking it would be easier to find the boundaries in a book than to find them on the ground, when she felt a spot of rain. Looking up, she saw that the wind was driving clouds across the sky. The spell of bright weather was over, and it looked as though it was about to rain in earnest.

"I think we should turn back," she said.

He agreed. They wheeled their horses and headed for home, but they had come so far that the house could no longer be seen. Susannah glanced at the sky again. It seemed like only a few minutes ago it had been blue, but now it was already half grey. The light dimmed as the sun was obscured, and the air became colder. The first drops of rain were few and far between, but they soon came more thickly and the horses bowed their heads. As Susannah tried to control the chestnut, her hands slipped on the wet reins and her horse took advantage of it by trying to turn his head against the wind. She pulled him back on course, but he was becoming increasingly skittish, and he was shaking his head as the rain went into his ears.

"We need to find somewhere to shelter," said Oliver, shouting over the rising wind to make himself heard.

"I agree, but there isn't anywhere," she called back.

"Yes, there is. Follow me."

He wheeled his horse and began to ride away from the shore. She had no idea where he was going, but as he knew the estate better than she did, she had no hesitation in following him. The land dipped ahead of them, and in a hollow she saw a ruined farmhouse. There was very little roof, but what little there was would afford them some shelter. There was a blasted tree growing out of it, but the walls appeared to be sound.

When they reached it, Oliver dismounted in one lithe movement and then crossed to the chestnut, putting his hands round Susannah's waist. She gathered up her skirt then jumped down with his help, sliding from the wet and slippery saddle and stumbling against him as she did so. He righted her, but not before she had felt the hard muscles of his chest beneath the soft fabric of his coat. The contrast was like the man himself, his dual nature containing more on the inside than was apparent on the outside.

She was now standing facing him, and her hands were still resting against his chest. As though drawn by an invisible string she looked up into his eyes and the world changed. Instead of the two of them being on the open cliffs, a part of the wild and stormy landscape, she felt as though they were in a place far away from the real world. The look in his eyes made her pulse flutter. She had never seen a look of such burning intensity before. It lit his blue eyes with a flame, deepening the blue rim and brightening the centre. She noticed how long his lashes were, and saw the blackness of the lock of hair that tumbled over his forehead. It seemed natural when he took her chin between his fingers, as though somehow she had been expecting it, and even wanting him to do it. She felt their soft pressure, and her skin tingled. She saw his face lower towards hers, and felt his breath hot and sweet on her cheeks . . . and then he released her, and she stepped back as though she had woken from a dream.

She watched him lead the horses into the lee of the wall to protect them from the driving rain, and then she went into a small room at the back of the tumbledown cottage which still had part of its roof. Having tethered the horses he joined her, and they stood in silence, their conversation having evaporated. But the silence was not dead. Instead, it seemed a living thing, charged with some potent force that made the air round them start to crackle. There was going to be a storm, Susannah thought. Thunder rolled far off, and soon afterwards, lightning forked down over the sea.

She stood and watched it as it moved closer and closer to land, heralded by torrential rain. She was already damp, but the downpour found its way through the roof and wet her through. Her hair flattened against her head, and rivulets of water ran down her cloak. Her dress was soaked. The lightning flashed almost directly in front of her, but she felt a far more potent force behind her. She turned instinctively and found herself dragged into Oliver's arms. The thunder paled in comparison to the storm of emotions that consumed her, and the lightning was as nothing to the energy that coursed through her when his lips met her own. They moved over hers gently, tantalizingly, and then with more firmness, until she was lost in a maelstrom of new sensations. She felt his arms crush her more tightly against him, and revelled in the hardness of his body pressed against her own. She felt him pull her closer and she tangled her arms around his neck in response, until they were so firmly joined she could not say where Oliver ended and she began.

She felt his hands slide down her back, down, down . . . and then they stopped. The intensity of his kiss lessened and she began to surface. She took her arms from his neck as he pulled away from her. He remained standing facing her, looking deeply into her eyes, then raising his hands he pushed her wet locks of hair back from her forehead and held her face between his strong fingers.

"We should go," he said at last.

She nodded mutely. The storm was passing. Already the lightning was disappearing into the distance, and the thunder was no more than a distant rumble. The rain was slackening, its rushing torrent lessening to a pitter patter as it struck the cottage.

Still they did not move. It was not until a gleam of sun shone through the clouds that Oliver dropped his hands from her face, and they walked back to their horses silently, side by side. He helped her to mount, and without another word they rode back to the house. It was not an easy silence but a turbulent one, still charged with the energy that had gripped them in the cottage. Susannah did not dare break it. If she did, she felt she would not be able to control the things she said.

Oliver made no mention of what had happened between them, and neither did Susannah. She could not think how she had come to forget herself so far as to allow him to kiss her. She could only think that, having been a governess for so long, she had forgotten how to behave like a lady. She had gone out without a chaperon and ridden across the cliffs with a man she barely knew, and disaster had nearly been the result. She must never let such a thing happen again.

The grass was drenched and the going was slow, but at last they reached the stables. Oliver dismounted and held out his hands to help her do the same. Susannah bit her lip. She should not slide from the horse's back into his arms, but there was no other way to dismount. Holding herself aloof, and making sure she touched him as little as possible, she accepted his help, but she stepped away from him as soon as her feet touched the ground.

"I'll see to the horses," he said huskily.

"Thank you," she said, and her voice trembled.

She went across the stable-yard and back to the house. It was good to be inside. Some of the energy that had gripped her began to dissipate, and she felt she was out of danger.

She went up to her room and stripped off her wet clothes, then dried her hair as best she could with a towel, and put on a dry petticoat. She put a fresh gown on top of it, and pulled on her dry shoes and stockings.

As she looked in the cheval glass, she was surprised to see that no sign of what had happened showed on her face. She looked exactly as she had done when she had left the house. But she was not the same. She was changed, and it was Oliver's kiss that had changed her.

~   ~   ~

What had he done? Oliver asked himself as, having called his servant to see to the chestnut, he rubbed down his stallion. He had intended to lure Susannah into a flirtation to punish her for speaking scathingly of marrying him, but nothing more. Once he had demonstrated his power he had meant to let her go, but instead of stepping back as he had intended, he had found himself prolonging the kiss and he did not know how it had happened. He had been in control of the situation when they had set out on their ride, but in the ruined farmhouse he had been carried away by forces beyond his understanding. He'd been impressed by her ability to control the chestnut, and intrigued by tales of her unconventional childhood, and he'd found himself enjoying her company, but none of these things could account for the way he'd behaved.

Had he been tempted by the way the rain had soaked her hair? he wondered, as he remembered how it had clung to her head, changing the shape of her face and rendering it inexpressibly beautiful. Or had he been tempted by the way the colour of her hair had changed, going from a nondescript brown to a sleek jet? Or the feel of her waist in the circle of his hands? Or the scent of her skin? He did not know. But the fact remained that he had allowed himself to give in to feelings more overwhelming than any he had experienced before, and that when he had tasted her lips he had wanted to take things further—much, much further, down alleyways from which there would have been no turning back.

He must never allow himself to be alone with her again, he told himself as he finished rubbing down the horse. If he did, he might find himself drawn into a world over which he had no control, and that was something he did not want.

He covered the dry horse with a blanket. Then, seeing that Kelsey had finished rubbing down the chestnut, he left the stables. As he did so, the irony of the situation hit him. He had set out to toy with Susannah, but fate had been toying with him. He had thought he was in command of the situation, yet he had been like a child playing with a tinder box. He had struck sparks from it as a game, only to find that he had started a fire in earnest. And the fire had threatened to consume him.

It was with relief that he turned his thoughts away from Susannah as he returned to the house. He went into the library, glancing at the long-case clock as he did so. He had almost half an hour before Edward and James joined him, and he could put it to good use. He threw off his outdoor clothes, then took a log book from the desk drawer. He took maps, tide tables and a calendar from the bottom shelf and spread them out across the table, then he sat down and began to study them, making notes in the log book. He didn't look up until he heard Edward and James entering the room.

"You've made a start?" asked Edward, as he pulled up a chair next to Oliver.

"Yes. I think we should sail on Tuesday. The tides will be in our favour, and it will give us time to prepare without delaying matters too long. I want to be able to make one more sailing after this one, before we have to abandon Harstairs House for ever."

"Agreed," said Edward with a curt nod.

James studied the maps and tide tables, consulting Oliver's notes before giving his own approval.

"Where will we land this time?" asked Edward.

"Here," said Oliver, pointing to the map. "In Normandy."

"And is there anywhere for us to beach the longboat?"

"Yes. I know the coastline around the area. There are

several suitable places, none of which we've used before. It's as well to keep changing our route. Once we've accomplished our goal, we'll return as soon as possible. The less time we spend in France the better."

"We'll have to make sure we're not followed," said Edward.

"We've done this before," said Oliver. "We'll do whatever it takes."

"How about Tregornan?" asked James.

"I'll go and see him," said Oliver, rolling up the maps and putting them back on the shelves. "Now that we know when we're sailing, I can make sure he has the ship and the longboat ready for us. We aim to go there and back as quickly as we can, and the ship will have to wait for us."

"It will cost a pretty penny," said James.

"As always," said Edward. "But it's worth it."

The three men stood up.

"When do you intend to go and see Tregornan?" asked Edward.

"Tomorrow morning, early, before it's light. With luck, there won't be anyone around—no unfriendly eyes spying on our movements."

"Very well. I'll let Kelsey know what we've arranged. We're taking him with us again?"

"Yes. He's a good man in a fight."

"We hope it won't come to that," said Edward.

"But it's better to be prepared," said James.

"It is. I'll let you know if all goes well with Tregornan. I suggest we meet here at nine o'clock in the morning. By then, I should have everything arranged."

The three men went their separate ways. Oliver went up to his bedchamber and took a bag of sovereigns out of a chest at the foot of his bed. It would ensure that Tregornan made a ship available, and a second bag of gold on their safe return would make sure they weren't left stranded. Tregornan was trustworthy for a smuggler, but it was best not to test his loyalty too far.

Oliver put the sovereigns in his coat pocket. There was nothing more he could do now until the morning.

CHAPTER SIX

It was dark as Oliver walked down the drive, his footfalls soft and silent in the early morning. The air was crisp, and his breath made clouds in front of him. He was a dark shadow passing through the landscape. Dressed in black, with a cloak thrown over his tailcoat and breeches, and a tricorne hat pulled low down over his face, he merged into the night-shrouded background.

Once he reached the gates he looked both ways, making sure the lane was deserted. After turning to the left, he followed the lane for a mile until he came to a signpost pointing towards the village. He did not go to the village, however, but skirted it, making his way to a house that was set half a mile beyond it. It was made of stone. It had a chimney, but no smoke was rising out of it.

Glancing round again to make sure that he was not being observed, he approached the house and rapped on the door: three slow knocks, followed by three rapid ones. The door opened, and with a last glance round, he went in. He found himself in a familiar room, some fifteen feet square, lit by tallow candles. The walls were of stone, and the floor was of packed mud. There was an upturned barrel at one side of the room, flanked by two chairs, and in front of the empty grate sat a roughly-dressed man smoking a clay pipe.

Behind him, unseen hands closed the door.

"Tregornan," said Oliver with a nod.

The man nodded in return.

"So you be needing my 'elp again?" he asked.

Oliver took the bag of gold out of his greatcoat and threw it into the air, catching it again with one hand. It jingled as it rose and fell. Tregornan appeared unmoved by the gesture, but Oliver caught the glint of avarice in his eye. Tregornan nodded towards the upturned barrel and Oliver put the bag of gold on top of it.

"We need the ship and the longboat, fully crewed, and no questions asked," said Oliver.

"You've no need to worry about that. Reckon we both like to mind our own business. Well, when do you want 'em, and where?"

"On Tuesday. Three coves west from the last time. We'll sail with the tide."

Tregornan took the pipe out of his mouth. "At midnight, then. And coming back?"

"No more than three days later. Possibly less. There'll be another bag of gold if you get us home safely."

"Not a trustin' man, are you?" asked Tregornan.

"I trust your love of money," Oliver said.

Tregornan nodded slowly. Then he spat on his hand and held it out. Oliver took it. They shook hands, and the deal was made.

Oliver went over to the door. In the shadows stood a mountain of a man with thighs like tree trunks and hands like knotted oak, who opened the door, and Oliver went out. He looked up at the sky. It was still dark. Good. He would be back at Harstairs House before the sun rose.

He skirted the village again, but no sooner had he passed it than three figures loomed out of the darkness and blocked his way. By their red coats, they were members of the militia. He didn't check his stride, but gave them a nod, and said, "Morning," before walking past. But his muscles were taut, ready for action, and his fists were clenched at his side. His ears were straining for any sound, and he caught it, a sudden twist of feet on dry grass. He stepped to the side, as a musket, wielded as a club, whisked past his face. If he had not moved, it would have landed with a crack on his skull.

He turned to face his attackers. What were they doing

here? he wondered, as he fended off a blow from the first. Were they in search of the reward Duchamp had placed on his head? And if so, how did they know where to find him?

He fended off a blow from the second, countering with a punch that left his adversary winded, then moved in and knocked the musket out of the third man's hand. But he was being attacked again by the first. He fought his way clear, punching and weaving with the skill of a boxer, but when he staggered backwards the second man tripped him and he stumbled. Regaining his footing, he fought his way free, only to find that his first adversary was swinging a musket again. Jumping back, Oliver avoided it, but he was punched in the back and then pushed. He lost his footing and fell, and the three men pinned him down. Then one drew away and began to kick him whilst the other two held him fast. He pulled against them, shaking their hold, dragging himself away by sheer strength and lunging at the kicking feet. He held them tight and the soldier collapsed. Oliver rose, but he was badly hurt and he swayed as he tried to stand. Another blow from behind brought him to his knees again and he turned to face his attacker, raising his arms to protect himself from the next blow . . . which never fell. Out of the shadows came more men, dressed roughly this time, and silently they pounded the militia, until all three were subdued.

"We can't let them go," said Oliver to the mountainous man who had come to his aid, as he rose and wiped the blood from his mouth with the back of his hand.

"We'll take care of 'em," came the terse reply.

Oliver nodded.

"We'll see to 'ee, too," he said, viewing Oliver's face dispassionately.

"No. I'm all right," said Oliver.

He could barely see out of his right eye, and his clothes were covered in blood, but he was in one piece.

Tregornan's men nodded then departed, taking the three militia men with them.

The sun was beginning to rise. Oliver turned his steps back to Harstairs House. He would have to hurry if he was to escape notice. But hurrying was impossible. He had a gash in his thigh. Blood was seeping from it. He found it difficult to see, and the further he went, the more unsteady his gait became. He had to get back. He stumbled onwards, picking himself up when he fell. If only he could get back to the house . . .

~ ~ ~

Susannah rose early. She went down to the kitchen and put more coal on the fire then began to prepare breakfast. She was just setting the kettle over the fire when she heard Jim's cheerful whistle coming across the courtyard. She went outside, hoping he might have brought her a letter from Mrs. Wise.

"Mornin', miss," he said, as he put a pitcher of milk down on the ground and took a clutch of eggs from his pocket. "Got a nice bit o' cheese for you as well this mornin'."

Susannah took the eggs and put them on the kitchen table whilst he carried the pitcher inside, then he reached in his pocket and pulled out a slab of cheese.

"Do you have any letters for me?" she asked.

He shook his head.

"Bain't anything," he said. "'Appen tomorrow," he added cheerfully.

"'Appen," she replied.

He took his leave and she went back into the house. As she put the eggs and cheese in the larder, she thought what she should do with her day. She and Constance had made a good start on sorting out the house. They had checked the linen and begun to make inventories of the rooms in the west wing, but Susannah felt disinclined for household tasks. She made herself a cup of chocolate and warmed some rolls by the fire. When everything was ready she glanced at the clock, but decided not to wake Constance. Constance had had difficulty sleeping of late and might need an extra hour in bed. She ate her breakfast sitting at the kitchen table, and then went up to the sitting-room. She was just about to pick up a book of engravings, which she had found on one of the console tables, when she caught sight of the courtyard garden. It was fully enclosed, but it could be reached through French doors leading from the sitting-room. There were French doors on the other three sides of the garden as well, one set leading to the dining-room to her left, one set to the drawing-room opposite and a final set leading to the passage at her right, which gave on to the top of the steps from the kitchen. This latter door would be particularly useful in future, thought Susannah, as it meant that trays of tea could be brought straight into the garden from the kitchen in the summertime, without the servants having to go through any of the main rooms of the house. As the light steadily grew, she decided to go out and examine the garden, seeing how much work it would need to restore it to its former glory.

The air in the courtyard was still and, protected by the house, it was surprisingly warm. It would make a very pleasant place to sit in future, she decided, and she started looking forward to renovating it. It was some sixty feet square, and had a path running round the edge of it. Eight narrower paths ran into the centre from the points of the compass. In between the paths, small bushes were planted. They were dry and twiggy, but Susannah did not know whether it was because they had died back owing to the season, or whether they were actually dead. She would have to wait until spring to find out. Or better yet, she would have to ask

Jim's father! There was a sundial where the paths met. It was a handsome stone monument, mounted on a pedestal, and it was covered in ivy.

She walked down one of the weed-infested paths that led to it and tried to tell the time, but the ivy had encroached so far that it covered most of the dial. She began to lift it free, hanging it over the side so that she could see the dial's face. Just after seven o'clock, it said. It was surprisingly accurate. The long case clock in the sitting-room had chimed the hour just as she had left the house.

Encouraged by the improved appearance of the dial, she pulled the ivy away from the plinth and cleared a small space around it. As she did so, she noticed there was some carving on the dial's base. It was covered with lichen, making it difficult to read. Taking out her handkerchief, she knelt down and began to clean the lichen away. She ran her finger, protected by her handkerchief, in the grooves of the letters. T ... I ... M ... E ... A ... N ... D ... T ... I ... D ...

She smiled as she realized what the inscription must read: Time and tide wait for no one.

She continued with her work, using a different part of her handkerchief for each letter, until she came to the O. She had just cleaned round the groove, and was wiping the lichen from the circle in the middle, when she felt the stone give. There was a grating sound and she felt the plinth begin to move. She sat back on her heels in surprise. The sundial swung slowly to the side, moved by some unseen mechanism, and revealed a hole beneath.

Once it had stopped, Susannah knelt up and looked into the hole. It was just large enough for two men to fit through. Leading down from it was a set of broad, shallow steps which disappeared into a Stygian blackness. She felt her heart start to beat faster. It must lead to an ice house, or a priest hole, or . . . she stopped and strained her ears, as she caught the faint sound of the sea. Perhaps it led to the beach, or down to a boat house built into a cave beneath the house. She was tempted to fetch a candle, but the steps were green with lichen and looked slippery. It would be dangerous to use them.

Reluctantly she pushed the sundial back in place. It was heavy, but once she had started to move it, it swung closed on its own. There was no longer any sign of anything untoward about it. The garden was lit by the early morning light, and the sundial looked as innocent as the rest. She decided that once she owned the house she would have the steps cleaned and she would explore the area beneath the dial thoroughly, going down with a local man or woman who knew the tides. Perhaps Oliver was wrong about them. Perhaps they were only treacherous in winter. If so, then she meant to keep a boat, and what could be more convenient than reaching it from a set of steps in the courtyard?

She finished cleaning the plinth, revealing the full motto without anything else untoward happening, then she continued pulling back the ivy, clearing the path around the sundial. She stood up, pleased with her work. Already the garden was beginning to look more cared for, and it would be beautiful when it was done.

She had had her fill of gardening and went back inside, but she could not put the passage out of her mind. If she could not find out where it led to by going down the steps, then perhaps she could find the other end. As she had heard the sea it must lead out on to the shore, or perhaps into a cave. She had not seen any crevices or openings on her previous visit to the sea shore, but then, she had not been looking for them.

The hour was still early, and she resolved to take a walk down to the coast. If the tide was low, she would see what she could find.

Stopping only to put on her cloak, followed by her hat, boots and gloves, she went through the sitting-room and out of the front door. Barely had she done so when she saw a figure walking across the lawn towards the house, approaching from the direction of the village. She hesitated for a moment, arrested by something odd in the figure's gait. The gentleman, for gentleman she could now see it was, seemed to be walking rather strangely. Drawn by a feeling that something was wrong she turned her steps towards him and, as she drew closer, she could see that it was Oliver. His head was down and he was walking unsteadily. Then he looked up and saw her. He was still some distance away, but instead of smiling or acknowledging her presence in any way, he changed direction, walking in an oblique line towards the back of the house. She thought that perhaps he felt as uncomfortable about their previous encounter as she did, and that he was trying to avoid her because of it, but then she saw him stagger, and wondered if he was drunk. It didn't seem likely. It was early in the morning. To be intoxicated at this time would have indicated a drunken disposition, but she had never smelt wine or spirits on his breath when encountering him in the daytime before.

She began to grow uneasy, wondering if he was ill. But why, then, had he turned away from her? Unless he did not want her to know: men were often foolish about such things. Still, if he did not wish to see her, she did not feel she could intrude. She was about to continue with her walk when, out of the corner of her eye she saw him stagger badly and fall forward on to his knees. He stood up again, but his movements were awkward and he looked as though he was about to fall once more.

Abandoning all thoughts of continuing on her way, she turned her steps towards him. As she drew closer she became alarmed. His face was bloody, and his left eye was black and swollen. There was blood on his coat and a tear in his breeches running the length of his thigh, along which she could see caked blood.

"What happened?" she gasped, hurrying towards him.

"N . . . nothing," he said.

"Nothing?" she demanded. "You're black and blue." Her eyes ran over his face in concern. "How did you come by such injuries?"

"It was . . . an accident. . . . I fell," he said, speaking with difficulty.

"Let me see," she said, trying to turn his face towards her, but he pulled away.

"It's nothing," he said again, sharply. Or his voice would have been sharp if it had had any strength behind it, but it was so faint that she had to strain her ears to catch it. He tried to walk on, but he staggered again.

"You're hurt," she said, taking charge of the conversation. "Let me help you."

"No," he said.

But he did not have the strength to argue any further. He barely had the strength to stand. He was swaying badly, and his injured leg looked as though it was about to give way beneath him at any moment.

"Lean on me," she said.

She slipped round beside him and pushed her head beneath his left arm, so that it was resting across her shoulder. He was so weak that he offered no more resistance, but let his weight fall on to her, steadying himself in the process. She felt her knees sag and she changed her position slightly to take his weight more comfortably across her shoulder. Then she put her arm round his waist. She felt him flinch, and realized that it was not only his face that was hurt. His body must be equally bruised. She began to walk forward slowly, supporting him as he dragged himself along beside her.

What had happened? she wondered as they edged their way towards the side of the house. She turned to glance at him. His face was ashen where it was not covered with livid bruises. His mouth was swollen at one side, and it was swelling even more as she watched. It must have been a very bad fall, she thought. Perhaps he had tumbled from the cliff? But he had not been coming from that direction. He had been coming from the direction of the village.

She could not plague him with any more questions at the moment, however, so she must contain her curiosity. She would have to wait until she had helped him back to the house and he had been made more comfortable, before she asked him anything further.

The house seemed a long way away. She walked doggedly, with his weight heavy on her, and their pace was so slow that she had the alarming feeling that they were not getting any nearer. Gradually, however, they reached the stone building, approaching by way of the kitchen garden, and she decided to take him in through the kitchen door.

As they reached the house, she said, "Can you stand by yourself? I have to open the door."

"I think so," he said, through clenched teeth.

She slipped out from under him, helping him to lean heavily against the door jamb before opening the door, then she assisted him into the kitchen, where he collapsed into a chair. She did not like his colour. Going into the larder she took a bottle of whisky down from the shelf, where it was kept next to the bottles of sherry, wine and Madeira that were used in cooking. She took the whisky back into the kitchen, poured some into a glass, and held it to Oliver's lips.

"Here, drink this," she said. "It will give you strength."

He took a little of the spirit before his head fell back again. She waited a minute, and then held it to his lips again, and this time he finished it. Some of his colour began to return. She put the glass down and set the kettle over the fire, finding a bowl and cloth whilst she waited for the water to boil. Once it was hot enough she poured it out, adding cold water from a bucket by the door until it was a comfortable temperature. Then, taking up the cloth, she began to wipe his face. She worked as gently as she could but he still winced as the cloth touched his cuts and bruises.

"I'm sorry. I'm trying not to hurt you," she said sympathetically, "but your wounds have to be cleaned."

"It's all right. You have a gentle touch," he said with an attempt at a smile.

As she wiped the blood from his face she saw that some of the cuts were deep and she found they would not stop bleeding. She held the cloth over them, pressing against them slightly until at last the blood stopped flowing. Wringing out the cloth, the water in the bowl ran red. She emptied it out and was just filling it again when Constance entered the room with a bundle of torn sheets in her arms.

"Good gracious," she said, her eyes widening in alarm. "Whatever has happened?"

"Mr. Bristow has been hurt," said Susannah, looking up. "He has had a bad fall. He needs a doctor."

"I will go for one directly," Constance said, setting her sheets down on the chair and unfastening her apron.

Oliver's hand raised as though to grip Susannah's wrist, but then it fell back to his side again.

"No, no doctor," he said in a faint voice.

"You might have broken bones," said Susannah. "I don't like the look of your wrist, and some of your ribs might be cracked. You must have medical attention."

"K . . . Kelsey," he said.

"Your servant?" asked Susannah.

"Yes. Fetch . . . Kelsey."

She looked at Constance.

"Find Kelsey, and bring him here as quickly as you can.

He will probably be in the stables. If not, look for him in the library."

Constance nodded and hurried out of the kitchen.

Susannah started to fill the bowl again, but a hand on her arm arrested her attention. Oliver had regained some of his strength and he was sitting upright. His eyes looked straight into her own.

"Not . . . much . . ." he said.

"Hush," said Susannah, kneeling down beside him. "You are too weak to speak."

"Not . . . much . . . time," he said, through swollen lips. "Say nothing . . . of this . . . to . . . anyone."

"But a doctor . . ."

"P . . . promise . . . me. No . . . doctors."

He seemed so concerned that at last she said, "Very well."

Once Kelsey arrived, she was sure that the two of them together could persuade him to see a medical man, or perhaps Kelsey might know enough to tell if any of Oliver's bones were broken. He lay back and closed his eyes, but he seemed easier now that he had her word she would tell no one.

She looked at his leg. It would be indelicate of her to clean it, but a practical streak in her nature, enhanced by her unconventional childhood, overrode her qualms. She raised his leg, setting his foot on a stool, then filled the bowl again and began wiping the cut on his thigh.

Soon there came the sound of footsteps hurrying along the stone corridor, and two men entered. One was James, the other was a short, stocky man of some thirty years of age, with broad shoulders and thick-set limbs. Kelsey, thought Susannah. Constance came behind them.

Kelsey took one look at Oliver and said to Susannah, "Out."

"You will need help," said Susannah, continuing to sponge Oliver's leg.

Kelsey knelt down next to him.

"Get out," he said to Susannah.

"You must forgive Kelsey. He doesn't mean to be rude, but Oliver looks to be badly hurt," said James, in a more conciliatory fashion. "He will need to be undressed if we are to tend to him properly."

Susannah bit her lip and stood up.

"Of course," she said reluctantly, for although she knew that what he said was true, she still had an urge to help. "Constance and I will be in the sitting-room if you need us."

"Thank you. We will call you if you can be of assistance. And thank you for taking care of him so well," he added, as Susannah and Constance went over to the door.

"It was nothing," said Susannah.

She and Constance went out of the kitchen, closing the door behind them.

"Poor Mr. Bristow! What happened?" asked Constance in concern.

"I don't know," said Susannah. "Only that he had some kind of fall. I came across him in the garden. He was finding it difficult to walk, and he was obviously badly hurt, too badly to tell me what had happened. I helped him back to the house and I did what I could to clean his wounds. But I am glad his friends are here. They will be able to make him more comfortable."

"Do you not think a doctor . . ." began Constance.

"I would rather he had one, but it is for his friends to decide."

"What a dreadful thing to happen," said Constance, shaking her head as they went into the sitting-room. "And such a nice young man. But let us hope there are no bones broken. He will probably be all right by the morning."

"I'm sure he will," said Susannah brightly.

She did not want Constance to know how badly it had shaken her to see Oliver in such a state. She had tried to tell herself that she didn't have any feelings for him, but seeing him in pain had made her aware of just how strong those feelings were, and although she took up a book of engravings as they settled themselves in the sitting-room, she found it impossible to concentrate. She could see nothing but Oliver in her mind's eye, with his dreadful bruises, and his pale face.

~ ~ ~

"What happened?" asked James, as Kelsey took out a knife and split the fabric of Oliver's breeches once the ladies had departed.

"I was . . . set upon," said Oliver.

"Who by?" asked James.

"Militia."

"Militia?" said James, sharply.

Oliver winced as Kelsey pulled the fabric of his breeches away from his wound. His leg was gashed, and around the long cut his leg was bruised.

"No more questions," said Kelsey curtly. "Not until I've finished here."

A look of frustration crossed James's face, but he nodded. He picked up the glass and sniffed it. "Whisky?" he asked.

"There's some kept for . . . cooking . . . in the . . . larder," said Oliver.

"I'll get it. How much have you had?" he asked, as he returned with the bottle.

"Susannah gave me a . . . thimbleful," he said, with an attempt at a smile.

"I'll give you rather more than that," said James. He half filled the glass. "Take it. You need it."

He handed it to Oliver, and Oliver drank deeply as Kelsey began to examine his leg.

"Is anything broken?" asked James.

Kelsey continued to manipulate the leg, asking, "Does this hurt? And this? And this?" whilst Oliver winced and replied in pain-filled tones.

At last Kelsey sat back on his heels. "No, nothing's broken. You were lucky," he said to Oliver. "You're hurting at the moment, but you'll mend."

"Thank God for that," said James, taking a glass of whisky for himself. "Now, tell me, Oliver, militia, you say? Where were they? How many of them were there? And what were they doing there?"

"They were . . . just outside the village. There were three of them. . . . No one of rank was with them."

"They could have been troublemakers, then, nothing more than men who wanted a fight. Or they could have set on you on purpose. What do you think about what happened? Do you think they knew what you were doing here, and wanted to take you to Duchamp in return for the reward? Or do you think you were just in the wrong place at the wrong time?"

With a second glass of whisky, Oliver was able to speak more clearly.

"I don't . . . know. It's impossible to say for sure. But whatever the case, they won't carry news of me back to Duchamp. Some of Tregornan's men had been following me to make sure I left—they were protecting his hide more than mine—and they dealt with the militia."

"And what of your mission? Did you manage to get

into the village and see Tregornan before they set on you?" asked James.

"Yes. They attacked me on the way back. Don't worry, it's all arranged. Tregornan knows when to have the ship ready for us, and where we want it. He'll supply it with a crew, as before, and no questions asked."

James's shoulders relaxed. "That's something. Even so, I don't like this new development. If our identities have been discovered, then we'll have to move on."

"We were going to do that anyway. We've only two more runs to make, and then we're finished here. After that, we'll find a new base elsewhere, and start again."

James pursed his lips. "I think we should cancel the run. It's too dangerous."

"We can't do that. It's all arranged. It'll go ahead," said Oliver. "But we must be on our guard." He winced as Kelsey bandaged his leg roughly, using his cravat. "Can't you do it any more gently than that?" he demanded.

"Perhaps you'd rather Miss Thorpe did it for you?" asked James with a grin.

"Curse you, James," said Oliver, but without rancour.

"You'll live," said Kelsey, finishing the bandaging and standing up.

"All the same, it was a pity Miss Thorpe had to find you," said James, as the bantering note in his voice disappeared. "It's a complication we could have done without."

"You're right," said Oliver, testing his leg by stretching and bending it. "It is. But it couldn't be helped. She saw me coming back to the house and I was too weak to avoid her."

"What did you tell her?"

"Very little. Just that I had had a fall. It was the best I could think of at short notice."

"And did she believe you?"

"No, I don't think she did. She looked towards the cliffs, and then looked back along the direction I had been taking. She's an intelligent woman. She quickly realized I hadn't been coming from the coast, but from the direction of the village."

"Then I'll have to tell her you had a fall from your horse," said James. He gave a wry smile, and his tone lightened again. "Be of good cheer. Something good might even come out of this, for you, at least. It should gain you some sympathy. The fair sex like nothing better than to minister to a man in need. You'd think blood and bruises would disgust them, but it makes them even more vulnerable to our charms. A wounded soldier, or an injured gentleman, it's all the same to them. After this, if I don't mistake my guess, she'll be ripe for the plucking!"

Oliver gave a wry smile, but he was not easy in his mind. He had seen the look on Susannah's face when she had cleaned his wounds, and his feelings towards her had recently undergone such a radical change that he had no intention of using his injury to draw her closer to him. He had no business trifling with the feelings of a woman who had done so much for him, particularly as he knew that without her help he might have collapsed outside. When his business was done, he'd leave this part of Cornwall for ever. Until then, it would be better for both of them if they saw no more than was necessary of each other.

But to his surprise the thought of their parting was more dreadful than the pain of his cuts and bruises.

~ ~ ~

Susannah was attempting to concentrate on her book, and trying not to strain her ears for any sounds from the kitchen. As she sat by the fire with her engravings, turning the pages at regular intervals, her thoughts were not tranquil. Oliver's wounds had looked dreadful, and she could not believe he had sustained them in a fall. But how else could he have come by them?

She stiffened as she heard sounds in the hall outside, and then heard the stairs creaking. It sounded as though someone was mounting them very slowly. Were James and Kelsey helping Oliver to his room? she wondered.

There was silence again, and then some ten minutes later a renewed creaking told her that someone was coming downstairs. Soon afterwards there was a knock at the sitting-room door.

"Come in," she called.

Her voice was surprisingly level, and she was pleased that it did not betray her agitation. Constance had already made too many comments about Oliver, and she did not want to give her a reason to make any more remarks.

James entered the room. As soon as she saw that he was smiling, Susannah felt a knot of tension inside her relax.

"I thought you might like to know how Oliver is doing," said James, as he remained by the door.

"How very kind of you," said Susannah. "Do, please, come in and have a seat."

"Thank you."

He sat down opposite her, in a wing chair, crossing one booted ankle over his other knee.

"It's very thoughtful of you to come and tell us," said Constance, putting down her mending. "We have been very concerned. Poor Mr. Bristow seemed grievously hurt."

"Is he going to be all right?" asked Susannah, trying to sound as though it was nothing but a polite enquiry.

"Yes," he said reassuringly. "He will be sore for a few days, but the wounds are superficial and there are no bones broken. If we can persuade him to stay in bed he should heal quickly but, knowing Oliver, he will refuse to be sensible and it will take a little longer."

"Gentlemen never like to fuss," said Constance. "My poor, dear father was just the same. He was attacked by footpads once on his way home from town, and although the doctor told him to rest, he carried on just as before. It was quite a week before he was hale and hearty again."

"How did it happen?" asked Susannah.

"He was thrown from his horse," said James easily. "A bird flew up in front of him, startling the animal and making it rear. He lost his seat and was thrown to the ground."

"Horses are tricky things," said Constance, shaking her head. "I don't ride them myself, and I am glad of it."

James smiled. "I assure you it is perfectly safe. Falls are few and far between. Oliver will be on horseback again before many days have passed."

Constance frowned, as though this was a foolhardy and dangerous undertaking, but said no more.

"And is his horse all right?" asked Susannah.

"Yes. It returned to the stables a short while ago, none the worse for its adventure."

"I'm glad."

James stood up.

"I must not trespass any more on your time. I'm sure Oliver will want to thank you himself when he is fully recovered, but for now, I hope my thanks will do."

"None are needed, I assure you," said Susannah.

"You are very good," he said, then he bowed himself out of the room.

"Well, that is a relief," said Constance.

Susannah felt as though a great weight had been lifted from her shoulders and smiled. She had been dreadfully worried, more worried than she had cared to admit, even to herself, but as long as nothing was broken then, as James said, Oliver should soon recover.

She turned her attention back to her book, but she still found it difficult to concentrate. For some reason she felt that James had not been telling the truth. But that was absurd. What reason did he have to lie? And anyway, Oliver's injuries had been exactly the sort he would have sustained if he had fallen from his horse.

"There, that's done," said Constance, laying her mending aside. "Another sheet to be washed, when Jim's sisters arrive. Are you content to look at your book, or would you like a hand of cards?"

"That's a good idea," said Susannah. "Shall we play cribbage?"

"The very thing."

Constance took out the pack of cards they had found in the writing-desk shortly after arriving at the house and the two ladies arranged themselves one on each side of the console table. They cut the cards and Constance began to deal.

Susannah picked up her hand. Two sevens, a king, a queen, a four and a three. Not a very promising start. But as she sorted her hand, she felt there was something strange going on at Harstairs House. It might not be haunted, but it was full of secrets. A passage under the sundial, an unexpected tenant, a mysterious accident . . . Susannah shivered.

"Let me make up the fire," said Constance.

But it was not cold that had made Susannah shiver.

Had Oliver really fallen from his horse? she wondered. And what was going to happen next?

CHAPTER SEVEN

Susannah saw little of Oliver for some time. She caught a glimpse of him from the drawing-room window almost a week after his fall, when she was taking stock of the furniture with Constance, and saw that he was looking better: his black eye had grown less noticeable, and his mouth had returned to its normal size. In fact, if it had not been for his limp she would have found it hard to believe that he had been incapacitated so recently. But after that she did not see him at all, for James found her and told her that the three gentlemen would be going away for a few days.

On the first night of their departure she slept uneasily. Although she and Constance had been careful to eat nothing that might disagree with them at supper time, she still had vivid dreams. She dreamt that she was rowing through a mist and every now and then she saw the beam from a lighthouse. It flashed regularly and she rowed towards it, only to remember that it was there to warn her away from the rocks, and not to beckon her to them. She woke up with a start, thinking she was going to row right into them, and was relieved to find herself back in her own bed. But the memory of the lights persisted, and she even thought she saw one flash after she had woken. So uneasy was she that she got out of bed and went over to the window. But there was nothing. Only the undulating mass of the sea heaving beneath the night sky.

Her dream had been inspired by finding the rowing boat, of course, and by the knowledge that she and Constance were, for the first time, alone in the house for the night. On the following two nights she slept more soundly.

"There's a letter for you," said Constance, joining her in the dining-room as the first light of dawn painted red streaks in the sky. "Jim brought it with the milk."

"Is it from Mr. Sinders?" asked Susannah.

"I don't think so," said Constance. "It smells of perfume."

"Then it must be from Mrs. Wise," said Susannah.

She put down her chocolate and took the letter. She examined the direction and saw that it was indeed from her great aunt's friend. As she unfolded it, several sheets of paper fell out. She picked them up and discovered they were pages torn from a fashion journal. Putting them to one side, she perused the letter. The writing was small, and the pages were crossed, but she was used to deciphering Mrs. Wise's letters and had no difficulty in making it out.

My dear Susannah, she read.

I was delighted to receive your letter and to learn that you are an heiress! It could not have happened to a more deserving person. I am very glad you are thinking of coming to London. Both you and your companion will be very welcome to stay with me. I am sending you some engravings of the latest fashions so that you can begin to decide what gowns you will want to order when you come to town. If you come to me in December, it will give you time to have a new wardrobe made before Christmas. The rage at the moment is for stripes. Striped skirts, striped bodices and striped sleeves are all the mode. Sleeves are worn long, gathered in at the wrist, and waists are tight. You will need a good corset!

Susannah read on, finally looking up when she had finished the letter.

"Mrs. Wise has invited us to stay with her," she said. "She will not hear of us staying in an hotel."

"Us? But I am not to go to London with you, am I?" asked Constance, with barely concealed excitement.

"Of course you are. I will need a companion," said Susannah, "and I cannot expect Mrs. Wise to chaperon me everywhere. That is, if you don't mind?"

"Mind!" exclaimed Constance. "I should love to go."

"Good. Then it is settled," said Susannah.

"But I did not know that you and Mrs. Wise were so well acquainted," said Constance. "I did not expect her to invite you to stay with her."

"I have only met her twice, but she says Great Aunt Caroline would have wished it, and that she is looking forward to welcoming us both to her house."

It was typical of Mrs. Wise to have included Constance in the invitation, thought Susannah, remembering her as a jovial, good-hearted woman. If the letter had come a week before, Susannah would have been looking forward to the trip to London wholeheartedly. As it was, she felt a certain reluctance to leave Harstairs House. London was the same as it had ever been, but somehow it had lost its allure, and Susannah would rather have stayed in Cornwall.

"Are these the latest fashions?" asked Constance, picking up the coloured engravings and distracting her from her musings.

"Yes."

Susannah turned her attention to the gowns that had been lovingly drawn and coloured for the pages of *The Lady's Magazine*. The gowns had the tight waists and long sleeves Mrs. Wise had mentioned, with small bustles padding out the skirts behind. They were worn with tall hats, ornamented with curling ostrich feathers.

"I can see I will have to have a whole new set of clothes made," said Susannah, comparing the gorgeous costumes with the gown she was wearing. "And you must have something new, too." She cut short Constance's protests by saying that she could not go to fashionable parties accompanied by a dowd, and Constance allowed herself to be talked round.

They spent a happy hour discussing their forthcoming trip, at last separating, with Constance going down to the kitchen to spend the morning baking. She had rediscovered a love of cooking since arriving at Harstairs House, and wanted to bake a seed cake.

Susannah had another plan in mind. She had wanted to visit the library ever since her ride with Oliver, so that she could see if there were any plans of the house: it would be much easier to find the boundaries on paper, rather than riding round the estate in an effort to find them. She had felt awkward about visiting the library whilst the gentlemen were there, but now that they were away it was the perfect opportunity for her to look through the library at her leisure. Not only did she want to see how far the grounds extended, but she wanted to see if there was any mention of the passage under the sundial. She had been unable to look for the other end of it, having been kept indoors by bad weather, but she was curious to see where it emerged.

As soon as Constance had left the room she made her way to the library. She had not visited it since her first inauspicious visit on the night of her arrival and she wondered what she would see. As she opened the door she saw a well-ordered room with a clean, empty grate. There were no glasses on the table as there had been the last time she had seen it, and no decanter. Instead these items were standing on a silver tray on the sideboard.

She looked around with interest. She had not had time to take in very much on her first evening, but now she was able to appreciate the size of the room and admire its decorations. She guessed that Mr. Harstairs had spent most of his time there when he had been at Harstairs House, for the room was more modern than the rooms in the rest of the house. It had evidently been refurbished quite recently. The pale-green paintwork was fresh, and the splendid white bookshelves that lined the wall to her left formed a marked contrast to the heavy oak used in the rest of the house. There was a large table pushed to the side of the room with chairs around it, and a desk, and two wing chairs were set one on either side of the fireplace.

She went over to the shelves. There were seven of them lined with books. In between the books were Grecian vases, and in the centre of the middle shelf there was a bust. It was of a noble-looking man with a wreath of laurels round his head. She looked along the rows of books until she came to a row with Harstairs House written in gold on the spine. The scent of leather drifted up to her as she took out the first one, but she was disappointed when she opened it. It turned out to be nothing more than a ledger listing expenses from five years before. She tried a second and a third, but they were similarly dull and contained nothing but accounts from years gone by.

Abandoning her search, she was about to leave the room when she realized she could put the time to good use by making an inventory of the room whilst Oliver and his friends were away. She went over to the desk, where she found paper and ink. She picked up a quill and, dipping it in the ink, she started to write. *Table,* she began, *chairs, sideboard, tray, decanter and six glasses, bust* . . . It was crooked, she noticed. She went over to it and straightened it. There was a click as she pushed it slightly too far, and a section of the wall sprang back. Her eyes widened in surprise as a dark corridor appeared beyond it.

So Harstairs House was full of secret passages! But why? The house was not old enough to have needed a priest hole, and it seemed strange that it should be riddled with secrets. It must have had a Machiavellian owner in the past, she thought, someone who delighted in cunning. She wondered if the passage joined up with the steps under the courtyard garden and was tempted to explore, but it was almost lunchtime. She would have to leave her investigation until the afternoon.

She pulled the door to, and there was a click as it settled back into its proper position. She went back to the desk and sanded her inventory, then folded the paper before tucking it into her sleeve.

With one last look around the room to make sure she had left everything as she had found it, she went over to the door . . . and saw the handle turn. She felt her heart skip a beat. The gentlemen were away, Constance was in the kitchen, so who was on the other side of the door?

She did not have long to wait to find out. The door opened, and Oliver walked in. His face had completely healed. The bruising and swelling had disappeared, and only a small scar over one eye remained to show that he had ever been hurt.

He stopped abruptly when he caught sight of her, and she was just about to welcome him back when she saw his eyes narrow.

"What are you doing in here?" he asked.

"I wasn't expecting you back so soon. Mr. Owen thought you would not be back until tomorrow," she said, flustered.

"I thought we had made an arrangement, that you were not to come into this part of the house?"

His voice was mild, but there was an underlying note of tension that made her feel ill at ease.

"I did not think it applied when you were not here," she returned. "I wanted to see if any of the books showed the extent of the grounds."

The atmosphere lightened slightly.

"And do they?" he asked.

"No, they don't."

"A pity," he remarked. There was a pause, and then he said, "If you have finished your search, my friends and I would like to use the library."

"Of course."

She felt awkward, and was anxious to be gone. Somehow he made her feel as though she had been caught in some wrongdoing, and she wondered why it was. Did he know about the secret passage? she wondered. Was that why he didn't want her in the library? As she pondered the question, a number of disjointed incidents connected themselves in her mind. She thought of the library as she had first seen it, with three half-filled wine glasses placed on the table and only one gentleman; the passage behind the bookcase; the storm lantern in the attic; Oliver's warnings about staying away from the beach; his choice of such an isolated location; the passage under the sundial; and her strange dreams of a light flashing on, off, on, off. Not a lighthouse at all, but a signal, seen in a half-waking state whilst she lay in bed with the curtains pulled back. Why had she not realized it before? Oliver and his friends were smugglers. She had thought she was coming to know him, but as she looked into the blue, glittering depths of his eyes, she realized she did not know him at all.

"What is it?" he asked, taking a step towards her.

"N . . . nothing," she said as her heart began to race. "Just that I am sorry to have troubled you."

Then, trying hard not to run, she left the room. But once along the corridor she broke into flight, not stopping until she reached the kitchen and closed the door behind her.

Constance's homely face looked up with a smile, and she felt some of her apprehension leave her, but a moment later it returned as Constance said, "I've just invited the gentlemen to eat with us this evening. It will do us good to have some company. They returned earlier than expected from their trip, and walked through here not five minutes since. I was planning to roast a joint of beef and I asked them if they'd like to join us. They were very pleased to have been invited. Their manservant will serve the meal, they said, so that we can all enjoy eating together. Won't it be nice?"

Susannah was aghast. *Oh, Constance!* she thought. What have you done? The last thing she wanted to do was to sit down to dinner with a group of smugglers, but if Constance had invited them then she could not undo the arrangement without causing suspicion, and that was something she must not do. She felt herself caught in a tangled web and did not know which way to turn. Should she tell Constance they were living with smugglers? Would Constance believe her? And if she did, what should she do then? Leave the house? Her spirit rose against it. It was her house, and if she left she would forfeit her inheritance. Besides, if she left, would that not be admitting that she knew their secret? If once they realized it was out, how far would she be allowed to go before they found her and stopped her?

Had she given herself away? she wondered. She had certainly slipped out of the library quickly, but could that not be attributed to the fact that she had wanted to fall in with Oliver's wishes?

Perhaps the dinner party was fortuitous after all, she decided. If she could be relaxed and at ease, and a good hostess, it might reassure any fears Oliver might have, for if there was one thing she did not want him to do, it was to suspect that she knew the truth. It would be dangerous. The best thing to do was to act as though nothing untoward had happened. After all, Oliver did not know what she suspected. He knew nothing except that she had gone into the library in search of a plan of the house, and if she kept her wits about her, that was all he would ever know.

~ ~ ~

Dinner would be an ordeal, Susannah thought as she changed her dress that evening. She would have to be at her best, and she had never felt less at her best in her life.

She checked her appearance in the cheval glass by her bed and sighed. She had had nothing new to wear for years and her dress bore no resemblance to the stunning gowns in the fashion plates Mrs. Wise had sent her. It was a serviceable gown in an unbecoming shade of mustard, which had once been a jaunty shade of yellow. Its three-quarter length sleeves were ornamented with lace that had once been fine, but was now mended in a dozen places. It had a square-necked bodice which fitted closely down to her waist, then the skirt opened to reveal her cream petticoat beneath.

She brushed her hair then began to arrange it, hoping an elaborate style would help to give her confidence. She piled it high on the back of her head, giving it fullness with three small pads, and allowing one thick swathe to fall free. She brushed the swathe, then arranged it to drape over her shoulder.

Well, she had done what she could, she thought, as she surveyed the results of her handiwork. She pinched her cheeks to put some colour into them and then went downstairs. Constance was already in the dining-room, checking that the silver and crystal were properly arranged.

"It was very kind of the gentlemen to lend us the services of Kelsey," said Constance, "but he is more used to looking after horses than setting a table, and the places were rather odd. He seemed to think we needed no more than one knife apiece, and when I reminded him about the napkins he looked startled. Do you know, I don't believe he had ever seen one before!"

"Is there anything more to be done?" asked Susannah.

"No, everything is ready. We are just waiting for the gentlemen to arrive."

There was the sound of footsteps coming across the hall and on the stroke of six the gentlemen joined them.

They exchanged greetings, and then took their places at the table. Constance had already placed the soup tureen in the centre of the table, as she did not trust Kelsey to serve it properly, and the gentlemen helped the ladies to a plate before helping themselves.

"It is very good of you to invite us," said Edward, as he picked up his spoon. "It makes a change for us to have such charming company."

"It is good for us, too," said Constance. "Miss Thorpe and I have been plagued by strange dreams lately, and we feared the solitude had been preying on our nerves. I dreamt the king and queen paid us a visit, and only a few nights ago Miss Thorpe dreamt that she saw a light flashing on and off out at sea."

"Did she indeed?" asked Oliver.

Susannah wished Constance had not picked on that subject, particularly when Oliver turned to look at her keenly. She avoided his eye and kept her attention fixed firmly on her soup.

"Did you discover the cause of the flashing light?" he asked her.

She raised her head and tried to speak lightly.

"It was a lighthouse. But let us not talk of dreams," she said, changing the subject to the safest one she could think of. "It was rather colder today, I thought."

"Oh, yes, there was a chill in the air," Constance agreed. "You have been here since June, I understand," she went on, turning to Edward. "How is the weather in the summer? Is it as wet as it has been recently?"

"There was some rain, but we also had plenty of sun."

"It must be lovely in the summertime," mused Constance. "It would be nice to be free of the draughts. When we first came here we were warned that Harstairs House was haunted, but I think it's the chill wind that has made people believe so. It can be very disconcerting to feel a breeze coming from nowhere."

"I don't believe you've anything to fear," said Edward gallantly. "We've seen no sign of ghosts."

"As soon as I saw the house, I thought there would be nothing to worry about," said Constance. "It's not old enough to have ghosts. The only thing we'll have to worry about, so close to the sea, will be smugglers!"

Worse and worse, thought Susannah, as Edward shot a sharp glance at Constance. She tried to continue eating, but her throat was constricted and her heart was beating painfully in her chest.

"Indeed?" said Edward.

To Susannah's sensitized ears the question seemed loaded with danger.

"Yes, indeed. Our village had frequent visits from smugglers when I was a girl. They came to supply the parson with brandy! Of course, he shouldn't have bought it, but he turned a blind eye to the parishioners' faults and they turned a blind eye to his."

"Ah! You don't disapprove, then?" asked Edward.

"I'm sure I don't know enough about it to approve or disapprove," said Constance. "I suppose we should all pay our taxes, but I can't see why the government should make quite so much money out of spirits when they do nothing to make them or bring them into the country."

"An enlightened view," said Edward with a wry smile.

"And you?" asked Oliver, turning to Susannah.

She had remained quiet throughout the discussion, silently willing Constance to turn the conversation towards London, the house, the refurbishments they had in mind, the weather, the gentlemen's horses, in fact anything but smuggling. But now she had been asked a direct question she could not fail to reply.

"I cannot approve," she said. "But as long as no one is hurt in the enterprise, then I see no reason to interfere."

"I see."

His long fingers closed round the stem of his wine glass. They were fine and tapering, but possessed of great strength for all that, and she thought they could be dangerous if he chose. Her reply had given nothing away, but if he suspected she knew, then she hoped her words would act as a warning to him.

"Well said," agreed Edward.

Constance, finally sensing that something was not quite right, looked from one to the other of them.

"If we have all finished our soup, I think we should move on to the beef," said Susannah.

There was a round of agreement. The soup plates were cleared and the sirloin of beef was brought in. Edward carved, and whilst he did so, Susannah took a firm hold on the conversation, asking the gentlemen about their experiences of London and the Grand Tour.

As James regaled them with an account of his adventures in Italy, Susannah felt Oliver's eyes on her, but could not read his expression. Was it of a man at ease with the world, or was it the look of a predator cornered?

"We will be going to London ourselves, soon," said Constance. "One of Miss Thorpe's friends has kindly invited us to stay with her."

"Indeed?" asked James politely. "You will not be going too soon, I hope? We would be sorry to see you go."

"We will not be going until I have spent a month in Harstairs House," said Susannah, "but once I've fulfilled the terms of Mr. Harstairs's will, then we will go straight away."

"Ah." James seemed to relax. "Then we will be leaving before you, although I am beginning to wish we could stay. Our time here has been so much more pleasant with some female company."

"You are too kind," said Susannah.

"I think you are wise to go away for the winter," said Edward. "The storms can be fierce, and there is very little to do here when the nights are dark. It is different in London, of course."

Susannah gave an inward sigh of relief as she was able to turn the conversation towards the joys of London, and they talked of the galleries and parks, the theatres and shops, until the candles burnt down low.

"I think we should withdraw," said Susannah, as they finished their meal with a whipped syllabub.

"No," said Edward, rising. "I think on this occasion it is we who should withdraw. Thank you for inviting us to dine with you. It has been a most enjoyable evening, but now we will bid you good night."

The gentlemen rose. Oliver cast Susannah a searching

glance before he followed Edward and James out of the room.

Does he know what I suspect? she thought, as the door closed behind him. She could only hope that he didn't.

"A delightful evening," said Constance. "Such charming gentlemen. I will be quite sorry when they go. There is no doubt about it, the house will be lonelier without them. It has been a comfort to know they are near at hand, for we are so very isolated here."

"But we will have Jim with us, and his father," said Susannah bracingly. "Perhaps they might be persuaded to live here. They could sleep above the stables."

"Oh, yes, that would be a comfort," said Constance. "I only hope that Mr. Sinders knows nothing against them, and that they prove to be satisfactory. It will make things so much easier if we have a few men about the house."

The ladies retired soon after the gentlemen had left. As Susannah returned to her room, she thought the evening had passed off as well as could be expected, but the question remained, now that she suspected Oliver of smuggling, what was she going to do about it?

CHAPTER EIGHT

Susannah passed a restless night and woke feeling unre-
freshed. She was no closer to deciding what she should do
about the problem of Oliver and his friends than she had
been the night before. She made a poor breakfast, forcing down a few morsels of cake and a cup of chocolate. It
was by no means certain the gentlemen were smugglers,
she reminded herself, for although she had her suspicions,
she did not know if they were correct. She had convinced
herself that she had seen someone signalling out to sea in
the small hours of the morning because she had dreamt
of a lighthouse, and she had assumed that Oliver's friends
had disappeared into the secret passage in the library when
she had first arrived at the house because their glasses had
been on the table, but her dream could just have been a

dream, and the gentlemen could have been searching the rest of the house in order to find the cause of the noise they heard. They might not even know the passage existed, let alone be guilty of using it for nefarious purposes. Her other suspicions were built on similarly shifting foundations. The only things she knew to be real, and not the product of an overactive imagination, were the passages.

"It's a fine morning," said Constance, breaking into her thoughts. "The gentlemen have made the most of it and gone riding. I saw them in the yard, and they told me they mean to be out until lunchtime. I have been so busy that I have neglected my exercise of late, but I think I will take a walk this morning. Will you join me?"

Susannah put down her cup of chocolate. Constance's words had given her an idea. If the gentlemen were out of the way, then she must explore the passages. The steps underneath the sundial had been slippery, and she thought it would be dangerous to go down them, for if she was not careful she could fall into the sea, which she had heard below. But the passage in the library had been clean and dry, and it would be easy to find out where it led.

"No, I don't think so," she said. "I have some things I would like to attend to around the house."

Once Constance had departed, however, she hesitated. Would it not be better to wait until she inherited the house, and then she could explore the passages with an army of footmen at her back? But by then, it might be too late. If Harstairs House was indeed being used for smuggling, then it was possible that she and Constance might be in danger, and she needed to know straight away.

She thought over the meal the evening before. Could Oliver, Edward and James really be dangerous? On the surface it seemed unlikely. They were all charming. But underneath? There was a streak of ruthlessness in Oliver, and possibly in the other men as well. Then there was Oliver's unexplained accident. What if it had not been an accident? What if it had been as a result of a fight with excise men?

Deciding that she would have no peace unless she found out the truth, she made up her mind to search the passages. Should she tell Constance what she intended? she wondered, then decided against it. She did not want to worry her friend, and besides, she would feel very foolish if the passage turned out to lead to nothing more than a large store cupboard! But in case she found herself in difficulties, she decided to leave Constance a note. If she should disappear, she knew Constance would eventually look for her in her bedchamber.

Going into the sitting-room, she sat down at the writing table. She took up a quill and composed a letter, sanding and folding it before taking it upstairs and leaving it on her bedside table with a direction for Constance to open it when it was dark. Picking up her fob watch she slipped it in her pocket so that she could make sure she did not stay too long in the passage, then she went into the library.

It was warm. The fire was burning in the grate and, bathed in sunshine, the room looked peaceful. But appearances could be deceptive. Susannah took a candelabra from the mantelpiece and lit the three candles from the small flames, then turned the bust and watched the wall swing back. Cautiously she stepped inside.

The passage was well used. There was no smell of damp or dust. It was some eight feet high and six feet wide and, with a floor of packed earth, it was easy to follow. As she went on she walked with more confidence. Her candle illuminated the small space, giving her plenty of light to see by, and she saw the corner of the passage ahead of her clearly. She turned it and before her she saw a set of stairs. They were not like those beneath the courtyard, made of stone and covered in slime. Instead they were clean and dry, and made of wood. She went down. Twenty . . . thirty . . . she counted the steps as she went. Every now and then she came to a small landing and paused for a rest before turning and going down again. Forty . . . fifty . . . She began to hear dripping water, and the air grew damp. Another landing, another turning, another twenty steps and she found herself at the bottom, standing on a rock ledge at the back of a cave. The candles danced as a draught caught them, and she sheltered them with her hand. Then she went forward.

The cave had a sandy floor and rock walls, down which water dripped. Even when she lifted the candelabra, she could not see the roof. It must be somewhere above her, but she saw only blackness. There was a natural stone shelf around most of the cave, and on it were dozens of barrels. She went over to the first and examined it. It was made of wood and banded with iron. The other barrels were the same. They were all weather-beaten, and they were all empty.

What had she been expecting? she asked herself.

Brandy, she thought. Barrels and barrels of it. But there was none there. Moreover . . . she leant closer and sniffed . . . they did not smell of brandy. In one of them, she caught the faint whiff of something else, something acrid. She could not place it. For some reason it reminded her of being with her father, at night, watching . . . fireworks! She wrinkled her nose. She knew what the smell was. It was gunpowder.

She stepped back, alarmed, and almost toppled off the ledge. Righting herself, she fought down an urge to run back to the steps and instead went on. If Oliver was transporting gunpowder to France, then things were worse than she had suspected. He and his friends were not smugglers depriving the government of taxes, they were aiding revolutionaries.

She shivered. The cave seemed suddenly cold and

dank. She longed to be back in the sitting-room, or better yet, with the Russells, with only a cold attic and unruly children to worry about.

Chiding herself for being so lily-livered, she forced herself on. Suspecting Oliver was a revolutionary was not enough for her peace of mind. She needed proof so that she could take it to a Justice. She looked in further barrels but she found nothing of interest, except a remnant of a French newspaper dated a few days before, a date when Oliver and his friends had been away. So now she knew where they had gone. And she had seen the flashing light at the same time. It had indeed been a signal, and not just a dream.

The sound of the sea grew louder as she moved along the ledge, and she could see it lapping against the sand in the cave. There, moored in water just deep enough to contain it, was Oliver's rowing boat. His words about dangerous tides came back to her and she knew he had exaggerated. The tides were no more dangerous here than elsewhere, but he had wanted to keep her away from the beach, so that she would not see him putting out to sea.

She had learnt all she could from the cave. Making her way back to the steps, she climbed them hurriedly, wanting to get back to the warmth and light of the rooms above. But what then? She must put this in the hands of the authorities, but she did not know how to do it. She paused once on the way up as the steps were steep and made her breathless, but she ascended as quickly as she could. She emerged in the library and quickly shut the passage, then blowing out the candles she replaced them on the mantelpiece. Returning to the sitting-room she paced the room and tried to decide what to do. Should she leave? A glance at the clock showed her that it was twelve o'clock. Oliver and his friends could be returning at any time and if she left the house she might meet them on the road. They knew she had to remain in the house if she was to claim her inheritance, and if they saw her outside they would be suspicious, and even dangerous.

Should she write a note for Mr. Sinders and give it to Jim? she wondered. Or should she send Constance for help whilst she herself remained, hiding Constance's absence by telling the gentlemen that her companion had had a headache and had taken to her bed? Or better yet, saying that Constance had a toothache and had gone to try and find an apothecary in the village?

Her thoughts went round and round in circles, and she did not notice the passage of time, until she heard the door opening. She turned towards it, expecting to see Constance, only to give a start as she saw Oliver instead. He was looking larger than she remembered him. His hair fell forward, uncontained by a ribbon, shadowing his eyes. He was dressed in nothing but a shirt and breeches, and she felt her heart begin to race. He looked as though he had come to her in haste. She backed away from him as he entered the room.

"Mr. Bristow," she said warily, trying to sound as though she was at ease.

"Miss Thorpe," he said, his blue eyes glittering.

He shut the door behind him and stood in its way, his massive shoulders blocking it. Susannah wondered if she could slip past him and out into the hall but she knew it was impossible. He had cut off her route of escape. There was, however, another one. The french windows leading into the garden were unlocked and she could escape that way . . . but once in the garden she would have no way out again, for the other doors were locked, and she would be trapped there.

"What brings you here?" she asked, trying to bluff her way through the situation.

"The library," he said.

She lifted her eyebrows, hoping he could not hear her heart beating like a drum. "The library?" she enquired.

"Let's not play games," he said harshly. "You found the passage yesterday, and you went down to the cave this morning when we were out. Someone should have taught you to curb your curiosity. It's a dangerous quality."

Susannah swallowed. The air was full of peril. It sparked around her with a threatening intensity, making her feel vulnerable and afraid. She was alone in the room with him, and she thought desperately of how she could save herself. There was a heavy candlestick on the mantelpiece, but she doubted if she could reach it, let alone hit him with enough force to knock him out.

"How did you know?" she asked, playing for time. If Constance came into the room, it would be enough of a distraction for them both to escape, and they could barricade themselves in the kitchen.

"The candles had burnt down. No one would light them in daylight, unless they were going into the passage, and I knew that neither James nor Edward had been there."

Even through her fear, she was vexed with herself for not having thought of that. She should have taken a candle from the sitting-room, and then he would never have known. But it was too late to worry about that now.

"I have every right to go in there," she said, trying to turn the conversation around and facing up to him. "It's my house, after all."

"Of course. But I wonder what you made of what you saw?" he said menacingly.

"I made nothing of it," she said, but her heart was beating quickly, for he was dangerous and she must be on her guard.

"You suspect me of smuggling," he said. Then, as if reading her mind, his face changed and he said, "Or something worse. Tell me Miss Thorpe, what *do* you think?"

"I think it is none of my business," she said, wondering if Constance would hear her if she shouted for help.

"But it is. As you've said, it's your house. And so I think you should see for yourself exactly what it is I'm doing here."

"No."

She shrank back.

He moved towards her implacably.

"Oh, but I insist."

"There is no need," she said, stopping as she felt the wall behind her. Her heart leapt into her throat. She had nowhere else to go.

"There's every need. Come with me."

"No!"

"It wasn't a question," he said ruthlessly.

He took her by the hand and started to pull her out of the room. She tried to resist, but he was too strong for her. He dragged her across the hall, but when he put his foot on the first stair she began to be seriously frightened and she caught hold of the banister. Turning towards her with a pitiless face, he unfastened her hand with strong fingers, then sweeping her up in his arms he carried her upstairs, taking them two at a time.

"Put me down!" she said.

She pushed against his chest, but he ignored her struggle and shrugged off the blows that followed it. He carried her upstairs, along the corridor and into one of the bedrooms at the end, slamming the door behind him with his foot. He dropped her to the floor and she heard a grating sound as a key turned in the lock.

She looked about her wildly, expecting to see a group of filthy cut-throats looking up from their drinks, but the room was empty. At least that was one particular peril she would be able to avoid, she thought, as she turned back towards him.

"Let me out!" she said, shaking with fear and rage.

His eyes looked directly into her own. "Look at the bed," he said.

"Let me out!" she said again.

"Look at the bed," he said relentlessly.

She ignored him. As he did not stand aside, and as she realized it would be useless to try and get past him, she turned and swept over to the window. Flinging it open, she felt the wind stinging her face and she lifted the hem of her skirt, ready to climb on to the sill. Then she looked down. It was a long way. She scanned the walls for ivy, but there was nothing. The only way down was to jump, and if she did that she would land on the paving stones beneath. She would be badly injured, at best; at worst she would be killed.

Closing the window she turned to face him again, and saw that at least he had not taken any steps towards her.

He was still standing at the other side of the room. She felt her pulse begin to lose its tumultuous rhythm. If he did not make any threatening moves, then she should be able to escape yet.

Glancing round, she looked for anything that could help her. A poker on the hearth, a jug on the washstand—if she stood on the bed, she thought, as she glanced towards the four-poster, she could use the extra height to bring a heavy implement crashing down on his head. Her eyes went back to him . . . and then, her attention was caught by something she had seen, and she looked back at the bed.

His words had barely registered at the time. They had made no sense, and she had been too frightened to take them in. But now she saw that the bed was not empty, as she had thought it would be. There was someone in it. Curiosity began to rise within her, and questions crowded into her mind. Why had Oliver brought her here? What had he wanted her to see? And who was beneath the covers? She was afraid of what she might find, but inquisitiveness got the better of her and she went over cautiously to the four-poster. Under the covers lay a man. His breathing was laboured and his face was as white as the sheet. He was sleeping restlessly. She went closer, then seeing how ill he was she knelt down next to the bed. She put a hand to his forehead. It was clammy. Then she caught sight of something red beneath the sheet. Pulling it back a little, she saw that his chest and shoulder were bandaged, and that the bandage was soaked in blood.

"This man needs help." She looked at Oliver. "Who is he? What is he doing here?"

"He's no one," he said with a shrug. "A peasant, that's all."

She stood up. "He needs a doctor."

"No."

"But he must have one. Otherwise he might die."

"Kelsey has taken a look at him."

"Kelsey's a groom, not a medical man!"

"He saw to me."

"But you were not feverish, and your wounds were superficial. This man is badly hurt, perhaps he has even been shot."

He did not answer her implied question. Instead, he said, "Kelsey knows more about wounds than most doctors will ever do."

"I don't understand. Who is this man? What is he doing here? Where did he come from? What happened to him?"

Oliver joined her by the bed. There was nothing threatening in his movement, and she did not back away from him. He looked down at the injured man.

"You're right. He was shot. In France. He was escaping from prison."

She was puzzled.

"You mean he was a convict? I don't understand what he's doing here." She felt anxious at the thought of a possible murderer in the house. "What was his crime?"

"Something trivial. It is not necessary to do anything criminal to be imprisoned in France these days. People can be convicted without the courts hearing any evidence against them."

"Then you mean he's innocent? Poor man." She looked down at him again, wondering what dreadful things he had seen and endured.

"You don't approve?"

"Of what? Putting people in prison without trial? Of course not."

"But if it's to serve a greater good? If the end justifies the means?"

"Nothing justifies putting people in prison without trial."

She shivered as she thought of what was happening in France even as they spoke. Living in a remote corner of England, she had been protected from most of the dreadful details, but she had read the Russells' newspapers when they had finished with them, at least when she could manage to salvage them from their role as firelighters, and she was not entirely ignorant of what was going on across the Channel.

"Not even if a fairer society is the result?" he said, his eyes narrow.

"If," she said. "But I don't believe it will be. And even if it is, the kind of slaughter that is taking place in France is insanity." She looked at him defiantly. "So if you want to recruit me to your cause you will be disappointed. I want no part of all this bloodshed."

"My cause?" he asked.

"I had suspected as much," she said. "You are a revolutionary."

"And you like me less for it," he said with a satisfaction she could not understand. A faint smile hovered around his mouth. "Even though you know what it is to be a servant. Your life hasn't been easy, and you've had to be at someone else's beck and call."

"It's true, life is unfair, but this . . ." She looked down at the man in the bed. "This is barbarous."

"Then you don't wish you could send your employer to the guillotine?" he asked.

She grimaced. "Mrs. Russell was a tyrant, but she needed lessons in Christian charity, not a ride in a tumbrel. So, now, what are you going to do with me?" she demanded. "Now that you know I won't support your cause?"

The glimmer of a smile around his mouth broadened, and reached his eyes. It brightened them, making them warm and inviting. She choked back a gasp, seeing how it changed his face. The lines no longer seemed sharp. They had relaxed, making his face warm and appealing.

AMANDA GRANGE

"Susannah, my friends and I are not smugglers, nor are we revolutionaries. We are engaged in a far more dangerous enterprise. We are rescuing innocent people from France."

It took a minute for her to digest what he was saying.

"Then why did you ask me if I approved of the revolution?" she asked, puzzled. And then her face cleared. "You thought I might be in favour of it, because I had known what it was like to have to work for my living. You even thought I might have come here to spy on you."

"Yes."

"How many people have you rescued?" she asked.

"It's hard to say. Eighty, ninety, perhaps a hundred."

"So many?"

"To me, it seems so few."

She looked at him with a new respect, imagining him rowing his small boat out to a ship in the dead of night and then setting sail for France. It was a daring thing to do, but one that was fraught with peril. She imagined him making his way through France, liberating prisoners. . . .

"So that is why I smelled gunpowder in one of the barrels," she said. "You must need it for your guns. You store your powder in the cave."

"No. The cave is too damp. But we put the empty barrel there when we have finished with it, along with others already stored there."

The man in the bed began to mutter incoherently. Susannah went over to him and put her hand on his head. He was hotter than before.

"He needs a doctor," she said again. "Why won't you send for one? It makes no sense to rescue him from France and then let him die in England."

"We can't do anything to draw attention to ourselves," said Oliver, crossing to the washstand and pouring some water into the bowl. "He knows this, and he would approve of our actions. There is more than just his life at stake." He took up a cloth which was laid next to it, and carried both cloth and bowl over to the bed. He knelt down beside the feverish man and began wiping his forehead.

Susannah was surprised to see how gentle his actions were. He was a man of many layers, she thought. Ruthless when necessary, but he was able to be gentle, too.

"There are those who don't approve of our helping people to escape the revolution," Oliver went on. "If our purpose here is discovered by the wrong people, we will not be able to help anyone else. We have to move quietly, because if we are found out, then our lives will be in danger, and so will the lives of everyone we save."

"You said his crime was trivial?" Susannah asked, as the man in the bed began to quieten.

"He was a publican. He was accused of serving sour wine to defenders of the country."

"And that is a crime? How dreadful," she said in dismay.

"It is. Terrible. People are being killed on the slightest pretext, and anyone who dares to speak out against it is condemned as an enemy of the revolution and they are executed as well. Men, women and children are falling before it."

Oliver stood up and returned the bowl and cloth to the washstand, just as Kelsey entered the room, carrying a jug.

Kelsey looked from Oliver to Susannah and then back again.

"Where have you been?" asked Oliver.

"To get fresh water," said Kelsey.

"Very well. Then we'll leave Buvoir in your care."

He went over to the door and opened it. With one last glance at Buvoir, who was now resting more peacefully, Susannah left the room, and Oliver fell into step beside her.

"Will you take a walk with me?" he asked.

She hesitated.

"You have nothing to fear. I won't force you to go anywhere against your wishes again. But I had to show you what I was doing here, and it seemed the only way."

"You could have just told me," remarked Susannah.

"Would you have believed me?"

She thought of her earlier suspicions, that he was a smuggler, or even worse, a revolutionary. She hesitated.

"No. I didn't think so," he said. "I couldn't allow you to go on thinking we were smugglers. You might have told the excise men about the secret passage, and that would have been disastrous. I had to let you know the truth, and as you weren't about to go with me willingly, I had to make sure you did so unwillingly."

"I don't think the excise men would have troubled you, even if I had told them," Susannah said, as they went along the landing. "After all, I had no proof."

"You'd be surprised what they would believe. And also what they would be prepared to do to stop us, particularly as some of them might have discovered there is a price on our head."

His voice was dry.

She looked at him questioningly.

"There are many fanatics in France who are angry that some of their countrymen are escaping the guillotine. They want to recapture them if they can."

"The Jacobins," said Susannah thoughtfully.

"Yes. There are those among them who will go to any lengths to make sure the so-called guilty are executed. There's a Frenchman named Duchamp in particular who hates what we are doing, and who would very much like to put a stop to our rescues. He nearly caught us once before, when we were operating out of a house in Devon, and he made things so difficult for us that we had to leave and move on. But he didn't give up. Even though he didn't know our identities, he offered a reward for information leading to our capture. If you had alerted the excise men to our activities, there would probably have been one of them who would have heard of the reward and thought it worth his while to investigate, to find out if we were the men Duchamp was looking for."

Susannah was silent, thinking of all she had heard.

"Your injuries," she said. "Did you really fall from your horse or were you beaten by the excise men? Had they found you?"

"Not the excise men. The militia. They must have heard about the reward and, learning of three men living in a solitary house on the coast, they decided to see what they could find."

She looked at him sideways, as though seeing him for the first time. The situation was full of jeopardy, and yet Oliver was prepared to engage in it, risking his life to help innocent people escape from the savagery of the revolution.

They had reached the top of the stairs.

"So. Will you walk with me?"

She wondered if it was wise, but quickly dismissed the feeling. She was intrigued by him. What had made him dedicate his life to such a difficult endeavour? It must be a compelling reason, she thought. If he wanted to, he could have lived the life of a wealthy and attractive gentleman, drinking, gambling, and attending society's entertainments, where, as an eligible bachelor, he would have been feted and spoiled. Instead, he had chosen to bury himself in a remote corner of Cornwall and risk his life time after time for people he did not even know.

"Yes," she said. "I will."

Stopping only to put on her outdoor clothes she joined him in the hall. He, too, had dressed for the outdoors, with a many-caped greatcoat and tricorne hat. Together they went outside. The wind was strong. It blew Susannah's cloak about her, and tugged at Oliver's greatcoat. Susannah put her hand on her hat and set off beside him.

"You told me once that you did not know Mr. Harstairs, but you hesitated when you said it. Was it true?" she asked.

"I can see I am going to have to be more careful when I'm with you," he said. "I thought I had fooled you."

"Almost," Susannah admitted. "So you did know him?"

"Yes, I did. I told you that he made his money abroad. What I did not tell you is that he made a great deal of it in France. Some of it he made legally, and some of it he made in a less straightforward fashion."

"Do you mean *Mr. Harstairs* was a smuggler?" she gasped.

"He preferred the term free trader."

"So that is why the house is full of secret passages."

"Yes. When I began rescuing people from France I used his ships. He hired them out if they were standing idle. We came to know and respect each other. Then, a chance remark led to him being arrested."

"What did he say?"

"That he was a businessman, and didn't give a damn about the revolution. It was enough to put him in jail, and enough to have him executed. We knew nothing of this at the time. It was only when we attacked a prison that we found him and brought him home. It made our alliance closer than ever, and when our previous headquarters was discovered, he offered us the use of Harstairs House. At the time he was living in London."

"Do you know how he died?" asked Susannah. "I know very little about him, and yet his kindness has changed my life."

"He had a weak heart. He had had it for some time. His death came as a blow to me, nevertheless."

"How did you become involved with the revolution to begin with?" she asked him as they cut across the grass and walked westwards through the grounds.

"I know France well," he said. "I lived there for a while as a boy. My grandparents were French, and when my mother died I went to stay with them for a time. Have you ever been to France?"

"No."

"It's a beautiful country. My grandparents lived in a small village in Normandy. I used to spend my days roaming the countryside—when I could escape from my tutor, at least!" he added with a smile. "I loved France, and the French people. They were good to me. The peasants on my grandparents' estate were always pleased to see me, and I to see them. I didn't know at the time that not all peasants lived such comfortable lives—my grandparents saw to it that they had plenty to eat, and sound houses to live in. Those days were idyllic for me. But it wasn't to last."

He fell silent.

"I was too young to notice the terrible poverty or the growing resentment at the time," he began again, "and soon came back to England to be with my father. But once I had finished my studies I returned to France. I thought of settling there. It seemed to me to be superior to England in every way: the people were more cultured, the wines were more varied and the food more refined."

"Did you not see any signs of unrest?" she asked.

"Of course. But there was unrest here, too. I thought it was nothing more than a few dissidents making trouble and, like so many other people, I thought that once the National Assembly's demands had been met, things would settle down. That was four years ago."

"But they didn't settle down," remarked Susannah. "They grew worse."

He nodded. "They did. And I can understand why." He paused, and she felt a change in the air. It was as though he was dragging something to the surface that had been hidden for years.

"To begin with, I sided with the landed classes. My grandparents were good people, and I dismissed the tales of depraved nobles that were circulating at the time. I thought they had been invented in order to create trouble, until one day I visited friends of my grandparents. They were cultured, educated people, and they had a beautiful daughter named Angeline. My grandparents hoped I would marry her, and I was not averse to the idea. She was very pretty, her conversation was varied, and her accomplishments were numerous. Over the next few months I visited her family almost every day and I came to know and love her. Or so I thought."

He stopped, and Susannah did not know whether she wanted him to continue. To know that he had been in love with Angeline hurt her. As she thought of the Frenchwoman's many perfections, she felt the full force of her own lack of them. She was not beautiful, her education had been unconventional, and she expressed many views that a gently bred young lady would not espouse. She had no accomplishments, and she must have been

mad to think that a man like Oliver could ever feel anything for her.

But he kissed you, came the thought.

Yes, he had kissed her. But she had so little experience
of being kissed that she did not know if the passion that had
lain behind it had been for her, or if it had simply been the
result of a man starved of female company.

He began to speak again.

"There came a day when I was about to ask her parents
for leave to address her, but an incident changed my mind.
Angeline and I were out riding. She was a skilled horse-
woman and could master any horse. She liked to roam
round her parents' vast estate, and it was a pleasure to ride
with her. I did not have to hold back. She could match me in
speed and skill. We rode to the edge of the estate, and there
a beggar approached us. He was filthy and starving. My
grandparents had always treated such people with kindness
and I expected her to throw him a few coins, or to ask me to
do it for her. But instead, she lifted her whip and struck him
across the face. I thought she must have acted out of fear
and I was ready to reassure her, but when I looked into her
face I saw that she wasn't frightened, she was exultant." The
light had dimmed in his eyes, and his voice was hollow.
"She enjoyed whipping him, and if I had not taken hold of
her horse's reins, she would have trampled him to death.
She tore at me for preventing her, saying that she had a

right to do whatever she wanted to him. He was nothing but a filthy peasant, she told me, and deserved no better.

"I was horrified. To make matters worse, when we returned to her parents' house and she stormed inside, telling them of what had happened, they took her part. I went home sickened. If not for the goodness of my grandparents, my belief in the worth of the nobility would have entirely vanished. I found myself thinking that they did not deserve their power if this was how they used it, and my thoughts turned to revolutionary paths. So much so, that when the Bastille was stormed and the poor turned against the rich I was on their side—not in action, for I had returned to England by then, but in thought. And when I heard that Angeline's family had been arrested and sent to the guillotine, I shed no tear."

They walked on in silence. Susannah wondered what else he had seen and endured, and what other events had shaped the man who walked beside her.

"I almost joined the revolution myself," he said. He stopped, and looked into the distance, but Susannah knew it was not the cliffs he was seeing. It was the long-ago events he had witnessed in France. "Thank God I did not. It became more bloody with every passing month. It was losing its discrimination. Not only the bad was being swept away, but the good as well. I tried to persuade my grandparents to come to England with me, but they refused. They said they had done nothing wrong and had nothing to fear. They said they would be needed to rebuild France once the revolution had blown itself out, and I agreed with them. But three months later they were sent to the guillotine. They were falsely denounced in return for money, and they were butchered. I could do nothing to help them. I have never felt so helpless in my life." His voice was low and his hands clenched at his side.

Susannah longed to reach out and touch him, but he was wrapped in a cocoon of pain and she could not breach it. She had never dreamed that such a life lay behind him. It made her own problems of cold attics and unkind treatment seem insignificant.

At last he continued. "But I knew then that I must do something to help those trapped in France, and I must make sure that other innocent people did not share their fate. James and Edward felt the same way. They, too, had been in France, and had seen the effects of the revolution at first hand."

"So that is why you wanted a house here, in Cornwall, so that you would be in easy reach of France."

"Yes."

He seemed to pull himself back from a very long way away.

"How much longer do you intend to stay here?" she asked softly. "I know you have a lease on Harstairs House until the end of the month, but what then? Will you remain in Cornwall?"

"Cornwall, or a place nearby, until our work is done."

"Will it ever be done?" she asked with a shiver.

"In time. One day France will be restored to its former beauty," he said, his voice softening. He turned towards her. "You must go there, and see it. . . ."

The words *with me* hung unspoken in the air. His eyes looked into her own and she was lost. She felt herself being drawn closer and closer to him not physically, but in some spiritual way she did not understand. Nothing like it had ever happened to her before. But he was becoming increasingly important to her, and she found she could not contemplate the idea of a future without him. It seemed empty. Bleak. But with him . . . exciting vistas opened up before her, and she was filled with exhilaration. How wonderful it would be to go to France with him, when the terror was over, and to see the scenes of his youth!

But then her exhilaration faded. His life was so dangerous, perhaps he did not have a future.

"Are you never afraid?" she asked, searching his eyes. "When you go over to France? Do you never think you will be shot? Or that you will be caught, or that you, too, might go to the guillotine?"

"No."

"But I am afraid for you," she said.

She had never meant such an admission to slip out, but as he turned towards her she saw a look of such hunger and tenderness in his eyes that her heart seemed to stop.

"Are you?" he asked. His voice was low and throaty and his gaze searched her own.

"Yes," she whispered, meeting his eyes.

"Susannah . . ."

He pushed her hair from her face with the back of his hand, and as it traced her cheek she felt her skin burning as though caressed by the midsummer sun. But she could not give in to the feelings stirring inside her. She had allowed him to kiss her once. She could not do so again.

Seeming to sense her mood, he dropped his hand, and she stepped backwards.

"What will you do now you know the truth?" he asked.

"Help you, if you need it," she replied. "Constance and I can take our turn nursing the injured man, if nothing else."

He hesitated. "I would rather Miss Morton did not know about it."

"She is trustworthy," said Susannah.

"I'm sure she is. But the fewer people who know the truth, the better. A careless word could cause untold damage. She had not guessed, wrongly, that we were smugglers?"

"No. Otherwise she would not have talked about them so openly last night."

"It must have been uncomfortable for you," he said,

stroking her hair once again, and holding her with his gaze.

"It was terrible," she agreed. "But it led to this understanding between us, so in the end, I cannot regret it."

He smiled. Then he offered her his arm. She took it, resting her fingers lightly on the fabric of his coat, and together they went back into the house. They said nothing, but once in the hall, neither of them made any move to go. It was not until the clock whirred in preparation for striking the hour that Susannah stirred herself. By the lateness of the hour she knew that Constance would be coming out into the hall at any moment, on her way down to the kitchen to make tea.

"If you need any help, you will let me know?" she asked.

"I will," he said.

He lifted her hand and kissed her fingers one by one, then pulling off her glove he kissed the back of her hand, then the palm. Then, making her a bow, he withdrew.

Susannah heard the sitting-room door open, and she went upstairs. She did not feel equal to seeing Constance at the moment. She did not feel equal to anything but thinking of Oliver, and reliving the feel of his mouth on her hand.

~ ~ ~

Oliver was thoughtful as he returned to his room. He had never expected Susannah to find the secret passage, or to explore it, and when he had learnt she had done both he had been furious, and then afraid. Afraid for himself and his friends, and afraid for her. But his fear had given way to even more unsettling feelings when he had walked with her on the cliffs. He had been determined to avoid her, and to prevent his feelings from developing, but instead he had found himself taking her into his confidence, and almost taking her into his arms once again.

He went into his chamber, hoping to have some respite from his feelings, but instead of finding it empty, he found that Edward was there. He stiffened. By the look on Edward's face, there was trouble brewing.

It broke as soon as he had entered the room.

"What the devil do you think you were doing, taking Miss Thorpe to see Buvoir?" demanded Edward without preamble, leaping to his feet with a thunderous face. "Are you mad? If it turns out she's one of Duchamp's spies, then you've just given us away."

Oliver took off his gloves deliberately and put them down on the table, then removed his greatcoat and flung it over the back of a chair, followed by his tricorne hat.

He regarded Edward evenly. "She's no spy," he said.

"And how do you know that?" demanded Edward. "She turned up on the doorstep spouting a story about being an heiress—"

"You said yourself you believed her. Besides, you know

as well as I do that James wrote to his brother, who made discreet enquiries, questioning one of the clerks in Sinders' office, and it's exactly as she says: she'll inherit Harstairs House as long as she stays here for a month."

"If she is Miss Thorpe. Has it never occurred to you that if she is in Duchamp's pay, she could have waylaid the real Miss Thorpe and taken her place? It's not like you to be so careless."

"I don't believe that. I heard her talking to her companion on the first evening, remember, when I was about to go into the room and tell her we had agreed to share the house. They were talking about her inheritance."

"And was this before or after she said she would not marry you to save her life?" asked Edward, with a glittering eye.

Oliver looked at him sharply.

"What does that have to do with anything?"

"Only this, that you wouldn't be taking these chances if you weren't playing a game with her."

Oliver scowled. A game? It was a long time since his feelings for Susannah had been a game.

"Toy with her if you must, but don't jeopardize our business here," said Edward. "It's too important. You were a fool to take her into our confidence."

"What's done is done. Besides, she has offered her help."

"And of what use is that to us?" said Edward scathingly.

"She can look after Buvoir when we are not here, for one thing. I don't like the look of him."

"She'll never get away from her companion—or does the companion know, too?"

"No, of course not. But it will be easy for Susannah to say she's going for a walk or—"

"Susannah? So you're calling her *Susannah* now? By God, you're a bigger fool than I took you for," said Edward with contempt.

"Don't you have anything better to do than to argue with me?" asked Oliver dangerously. "Because if you don't, I can find you something. We're going over to France again on Thursday, and everything will have to be ready by then."

Edward walked up to him and stood within an inch of him. He was the smaller of the two men, but his look was pugnacious.

"Just make sure she doesn't leave the grounds in the meantime. Someone told the militia where to find you, and it could have been your precious Susannah. So tread warily around her, unless you want another beating."

Edward stormed out of the room.

"Damn!" said Oliver, walking over to the fireplace and resting his arm along the mantelpiece. Why had everything become so complicated? Not only did he have his feelings for Susannah to wrestle with, but he had another mission to finish planning, and now, to make matters worse, he had a split with Edward to worry about. Edward was as strong willed as he was, and on this subject neither of them was going to concede.

As if his present difficulties were not enough, his past had also begun to surface. Only now, when it did so, did he realize how deeply his experiences with Angeline had horrified him, and how they had hardened him to women. He had had enjoyable flirtations and a string of willing mistresses since leaving Eton, but Angeline was the only woman he had ever seriously thought of marrying, until he had discovered her true nature. And then it had set him against the whole idea, not only of marrying Angeline, but of marrying anyone. The thought that he might give his name to a woman and then discover her to be a monster had haunted him, but he had only realized it now.

And yet somehow, today, something had changed. He no longer saw Angeline as a representative of her sex, but as an individual—an extremely unpleasant individual. The look of compassion he had seen on Susannah's face when he had taken her into the bedroom had wiped the slate clean. He felt himself beginning to emerge from a darkness that he had not even known had gripped him, and walk into the light. The world opened out ahead of him and he saw a future again. Not as a collection of bitter battles as he tried to wrest men, women and children from the jaws of the guillotine, but as an undiscovered country full of promise. The reason for this rebirth was not hard to find: it was Susannah. She stirred him deeply, and not just his body, but his soul.

In Susannah he had met a woman with whom he could share his life, from the dark troubles of his efforts to rescue those in difficulties from France, to an afternoon's ride on the cliffs, and intermingled with his liking and respect for her ran a deep sense of unity and an almost overwhelming attraction. He could not believe that when he had first seen her he had thought her plain. She was anything but plain. Her eyes were singularly expressive, and were a gateway to the unique person beneath. But he had no business asking her to marry him, as he wanted to. His life was too uncertain. He embarked regularly on trips to France, and any one of them could end with his death. He could not ask her to marry a man who might well leave her a widow before many more months were out.

Hard as it was, he must face reality and allow her to go to London and forget him. He knew that she was attracted to him, and that they had a bond which allowed them to share their innermost thoughts and feelings. But once away from him, in varied society, she would have a chance to meet someone else she could fall in love with. She was young, and just embarking on life. She would have plenty of opportunities to meet and marry a man whose life was not so dangerous. The thought of her as the wife of another man hurt him, but he was no stranger to pain, and for Susannah's sake, he would have to learn to live with it.

CHAPTER NINE

Now that she knew her house was being used to rescue the French, Susannah wanted to do everything she could to help. She knew that Oliver and his friends would find it difficult to spare time to watch over Buvoir if they were planning another trip to France, and so she picked up her book of engravings and went upstairs. She scratched lightly at the injured man's door. It was opened cautiously by Kelsey.

"I have come to offer you my assistance," she said. "If you wish, I can sit with Buvoir until lunchtime."

Kelsey nodded briefly. He was a man of few words, and telling Susannah he would return shortly before twelve o'clock, he left the room.

Susannah went over to the bed. Buvoir was sleeping more peacefully than he had done the day before and his skin had lost its unhealthy colour. She felt his forehead. It was cool. Having satisfied herself that he was comfortable, she sat on a chair beside the bed and occupied herself by studying her book. He did not stir, and the morning passed quietly. Kelsey returned as promised, and she went down into the kitchen to help Constance prepare the lunch. Having enjoyed a cold collation they repaired to the sitting-room.

The weather was poor, with dreary grey skies, and Susannah had no wish to go out, so she and Constance amused themselves by drawing up an itinerary for their visit to London. They were just adding *theatre* to the list when there was a loud rap at the front door. They turned and looked at each other in surprise. Since their arrival at Harstairs House, the only visitor had been Jim, the milk boy.

"Who can that be?" said Constance.

"I don't know," said Susannah. "It must be Mr. Sinders, I suppose. He is the only person who knows we are here."

"Unless it is someone to see the gentlemen," Contance said. "They might have acquaintances in the neighbourhood."

Susannah thought this was unlikely, but did not say so.

"We had better answer it," she said. "I'll go."

"I'll come with you," said Constance. "This is a lonely spot, and it could be cut-throats."

Together the two of them went out into the hall, only to find that James and Edward were already there. Edward was opening the door and, as she saw who was standing on the other side of it, Susannah's heart missed a beat. There was no mistaking the distinctive red coats and the powdered wig of the captain, and behind him were seven more members of the militia.

"Good afternoon," said the captain, politely touching his hat. "My name is Captain Johnson. I wonder if I might come in and have a word with you?"

Edward stood aside reluctantly and let him enter. His men followed him, each carrying a musket.

"I didn't know there were any ladies here," said the captain, stopping short and lifting his eyebrows as he saw Susannah and Constance.

"This is Miss Thorpe, the new owner of Harstairs House. She inherited it on the death of Mr. Harstairs, and has kindly allowed us to stay until our lease expires," Edward said.

"That must be inconvenient for you, ma'am, is it not?" the captain enquired.

There was something behind the politeness of his words that Susannah did not trust. Why was he there? Had he found out that Oliver lived there, and did he suspect him of aiding French prisoners? Was he hoping to claim the reward by arresting Oliver and taking him to Duchamp? Would he dare do such a thing?

Outwardly, he seemed to be a gentleman. He was tall and well made, and his cream breeches and waistcoat were set off by long black boots and his scarlet coat. A wine-coloured sash was slung across his chest and the whole was enlivened by strips of gold. He wore a sword hung at his side, and his white-gloved hand rested on the hilt. Inwardly, he could be a Jacobin.

"Not at all," she said, answering his question. "The gentlemen have been most courteous. They are good company for my companion and I, and we feel the safer for having them here. Besides, it is useful to have someone to help us carry the coal and chop the wood. But won't you come into the sitting room, Captain? It's cold in the hall."

"Thank you kindly, ma'am. I will."

Susannah had been hoping that the rest of the militia would wait outside, but they followed him in and stood against the wall next to the door. They were not blocking it, but it would be impossible for her to leave unless they allowed it. She settled herself on the sofa and arranged her skirts around her. Constance sat beside her, and James and Edward took the wing chairs.

"Won't you take a seat?" she said to the captain.

"Thank you, ma'am, but not when I'm on duty. I prefer to stand."

"As you wish, Captain. Now, what can I do for you?"

"It's not actually you I've come to see, ma'am, though I remember hearing something about Mr. Harstairs dying and leaving his house to a . . . niece?"

Susannah let it stand and waited for him to continue.

He scanned the assembled faces, letting his gaze rove quickly over Constance and then move more slowly over James and Edward.

"It's Mr. Bristow I've come to see. But it seems he isn't here." He made it sound like an accusation. "Now I wonder where he might be?"

"He's seeing to the horses," said Edward.

"Is he, now? Then you won't mind if I send one of my men to find him. Norton is very good with horses. He'll be able to help."

"I'm sure he'll be glad of the assistance. Rubbing them down is slow work at this time of year," said Edward evenly.

"They do seem to take for ever to dry," said the captain good-naturedly. "Norton—" he commanded.

But before he could say anything more, the door opened, and all eyes turned to Oliver.

"That won't be necessary," Oliver said. "They've been seen to, although thank you kindly for the offer, Captain. All they need now is rest."

"Ah, Mr. Bristow. You have sharp ears, sir. I am glad your horses have been dealt with, because you are just the person I wanted to see."

Oliver crossed the room and sat down negligently, crossing one booted leg over the other.

"Here I am. What can I do for you gentlemen?"

"I'm here on an unpleasant task," said the captain with a frown, "and I regret it, but duty must be done."

He didn't sound as though he regretted it at all, thought Susannah. He sounded as though he relished it.

"Oliver Bristow, I have come to arrest you."

Edward and James exchanged glances, but Oliver remained calm.

"On what charge?" he asked.

"On a charge of smuggling."

"Smuggling? Aren't you out of your jurisdiction, Captain?" asked Oliver, his eyes steely. "Smuggling is dealt with by the excise men."

"We've been drafted in to help them. Loss of revenue is a serious matter, and the crown is concerned it is on the increase."

"And just what am I supposed to have smuggled, Captain?"

"The usual things, Mr. Bristow. Brandy and the like."

Oliver shook his head.

"I'm no smuggler," he said.

"Really? A cargo of illicit goods was brought into this country on 20th November, and one of the smugglers was recognized. It was you, sir. We have an eye-witness, placing you at the scene," said the captain.

Susannah felt her heart begin to beat faster. If the captain took Oliver into custody, there was no knowing what would happen to him. He had already been badly beaten by members of the militia as they had tried to capture him. He could be beaten again, or worse. He could be shot *whilst trying to escape*. She could not let that happen.

"The twentieth?" she asked. "No, that isn't possible."

She spoke pleasantly, smiling at the captain as though they were discussing nothing more important than the weather, but her heart was now thudding in her chest.

"No?" asked the captain, turning towards her.

"No. Mr. Bristow cannot have been smuggling anything then, Captain. He was with me."

"Was he now?" The captain looked at her shrewdly. "All day?"

"All day," said Susannah firmly.

"Well, now, that's very interesting, Miss Thorpe, but how about all night? Smuggled goods aren't brought ashore in daylight. They're landed under cover of darkness."

Susannah berated herself for having overlooked something so simple.

"The incident took place at three o'clock in the morning," went on Captain Johnson, well pleased with himself. "I don't suppose you were with him at that time of night, now, were you, Miss Thorpe?" He laughed jovially, and smiled at his men, including them in the joke.

But Susannah was not to be bested. She looked the captain straight in the eye and said, "Yes, Captain. I was."

"You were?"

"Yes."

There was a stunned silence. It was like a tableau, thought Susannah, as her eyes travelled round the room. She had seen one once, at Christmas time, when she had been a little girl living with her father. Some of his friends had dressed themselves in clothes from the dressing up box and had arranged themselves into silent groups portraying words and phrases.

This could be *shock,* thought Susannah. Constance's mouth had dropped open, her eyes had widened, and her hand had flown to her chest. James had turned to Edward, and Edward had turned to the militia. The militia had frozen in attitudes of frustration, whilst the captain's eyebrows had risen.

And Oliver . . . Oliver had not frozen. Like a real man of flesh and blood in an assemblage of waxwork figures, he was striding across the room towards her with a smile on his face.

What is he doing? she wondered.

When he reached her, he took one of her hands in his own. Sliding his free arm round her waist, he looked down into her eyes, and said, "Sweetheart, there was no need to do that." Then, turning to the others, who looked, if possible, even more surprised than before, he said, "You must be the first to congratulate us, gentlemen, Miss Morton. We were

not intending to announce our engagement so soon. . . .
Mr. Harstairs's death, you understand . . . but Miss Thorpe
has done me the inestimable honour of agreeing to become
my wife."

It was Susannah's turn to be amazed. She turned
towards him, eyes wide, but a squeeze on her hand reminded her of their danger, so instead of asking him what
he meant by it, she smiled, and looked self-conscious,
which was not a hard thing to do as she felt that if everyone stared at her for another minute she would sink into
the floor.

"Well," said the captain, breaking the silence, "so you
are betrothed."

"That's right," said Oliver.

"This is rather sudden, is it not?" asked the captain.

Oliver's smile widened. "Perhaps, but what could we
do? It was love at first sight."

The captain looked as though he would like to curse.
Instead he turned to Susannah.

"And you are ready to swear that Mr. Bristow was with
you on the night of twentieth November, ma'am?"

"I am," said Susannah. "I don't know who your infor-
mant saw, but it wasn't my fiancé."

"Apparently not." There was something in the captain's
shrewd glance that unnerved Susannah, but he did not
argue. Instead, he said, "In that case, I won't trouble you

any further. Thank you for your time, gentlemen, ladies."
He touched his hat. "Good day."

"Good day," said Susannah, inclining her head.

"I'll show you out," said Oliver.

He waved his arm towards the door, and the militia left
the room, with Oliver behind them.

"If you will excuse us, we have business to attend to,"
said Edward, making the ladies a bow before he and James,
too, withdrew.

"Well!" said Constance, clasping her hands together,
and turning to Susannah with a smile on her face. "I was
never more delighted in my life! I always hoped . . . such
a handsome man . . . but I never guessed . . . it was all
so sudden . . . but as Mr. Bristow said, love at first sight!
Oh, congratulations, Susannah, I'm sure you'll be very
happy."

Susannah did not like to deceive Constance, but she
could not go back on what she had said without revealing
everything, and that would be unwise. So she resigned herself to feeling uncomfortable.

"You need not fear that I will ever mention . . ." began
Constance, then trailed away delicately. "My lips are
sealed."

"Thank you."

"But you look tired. And no wonder. Those dreadful
men, bursting in here with their wicked allegations, and

then being forced to reveal . . . not that I blame you," she said, going pink. "It was most courageous. I will make a dish of tea."

She bustled out of the room, leaving Susannah to sink in a chair. She didn't know what had come over her. She had acted on the spur of the moment, fearing that if Oliver was arrested he might be shot, but she had never expected things to spin so far out of control.

Oliver soon strode back into the room.

Before he could speak, she said, "Why did you tell them we were betrothed?"

"I had to do what I could to save your reputation. I couldn't let you suffer in order to help me. But more importantly, why did you tell them you were with me on the twentieth?"

"Because I couldn't let them take you away," she said. "They have already beaten you once. Who knows what they would do if they had you in their power again?"

He sat down beside her and took her hands. "It was a very brave thing to do."

She felt his fingers warm against her own. "It was nothing," she said.

"No, it was something. A big something, and I'm grateful for it."

Grateful. She felt her spirits sink. She had not spoken in order to receive his gratitude. Gratitude was such a cold emotion, and her own emotions for him were blazing hot. But she could not let him know it.

"As I am . . . grateful to you for protecting my reputation," she returned.

"You mustn't be afraid that I'll hold you to the engagement. Once you go to London you won't need it any longer, as no one there will know about the night we supposedly spent together, and you can lay the blame on me when you tell Constance it's over. I won't contradict you."

Her spirits sank still further, although why that should be she did not know. He was doing everything in his power to help her.

"Thank you," she said.

"As for your neighbours here, they're unlikely to hear of it. I doubt if the captain is on visiting terms with the local gentry, and if he mentions it, once they know your engagement is over, they'll quickly forget about it."

"Because I'm an heiress?"

"It's the way of the world. Your neighbours will be busy trying to catch you for their sons. They won't want to blacken the reputation of a young lady who might become their daughter-in-law."

"It would be easier if the Captain did not mention it," said Susannah. "It's difficult enough with Constance thinking we are betrothed. I'm afraid she's likely to congratulate you."

"I can bear it," he said lightly.

"And what of your friends? What will they think?"

He pushed back a tendril of her hair. "That I am a very lucky man."

She stood up. It was exactly what she would have wanted him to say if their betrothal had been real. It would have delighted her. But it was not real. She walked over to the table, pretending to make it ready for Constance.

"Here we are." Constance bustled into the room. "I brought three cups," she said to Susannah, as she put the tray down on the table. "I thought Mr. Bristow might wish to join us."

"How very kind," he said.

Just for once, Susannah wished that Constance had not been so thoughtful.

"I must offer you my congratulations," she said to Oliver. "I have just been telling Susannah how delighted I am. You are very lucky to have won her."

"I know," he said.

She poured the tea, and handed them each a dish.

"It must have been difficult for you to keep it a secret, though I quite understand. It was so sudden, and so romantic. Love at first sight! What a pity you have not been able to announce it, but with Mr. Harstairs only just buried, of course it would not be seemly. When do you think you will be able to give notice of it?" she asked.

"We haven't thought about it yet," said Oliver.

"Will you tell Mrs. Wise?" she asked Susannah.

"No," said Susannah. "Not yet."

Constance nodded. "You can tell her when you remove to London. She will be delighted, I'm sure."

Susannah said nothing, but drank her tea. She was finding the questions harder and harder to bear, but they were perfectly natural, and if she had been engaged, she would have been eager to answer them.

Having finished his drink, Oliver stood up.

"This has been very pleasant, but if you will excuse me, I have business to attend to. My thanks for the tea," he said to Constance.

"It was a pleasure," said Constance. "Pray, don't let us detain you. I'm sure you must want to make sure everything is sorted out before your wedding."

He made them a bow then withdrew, leaving Susannah to contemplate the enormity of the web she had so hastily spun.

~ ~ ~

"At last," said Edward, as Oliver strode into the library. "We've been waiting for you."

Edward and James were sitting at the table, with their arms leaning on it.

Oliver raised one eyebrow. "If you have both been waiting here for me, it must be serious," he said lightly.

"It is."

Oliver sat down, sweeping the tails of his coat out of the way as he did so.

"You're a fool, Oliver. You've put us all in danger," said Edward angrily. "It was a mistake telling Miss Thorpe what we are doing here. I said so at the time, and this is the result. We're visited by Duchamp's spies."

"You seem certain about that. They might have nothing to do with Duchamp. They might be doing what the captain claims they are doing—helping the excise men rid the area of smuggling."

"Pah! They didn't even know what they were charging you with. *Smuggling brandy and the like.* They suspect we're the men Duchamp is looking for, and they're here because of the reward."

"Perhaps, but their visit had nothing to do with Susannah."

"Open your eyes, Oliver. She comes here with the disguise of being an heiress and installs herself in the house. Shortly afterwards, you are set upon by the militia and almost killed. Then she searches the library when we're out and discovers the secret passage. She spouts some nonsense about thinking we're smugglers to bring us out into the open, and you're completely deceived. You tell her what we're doing here. Even worse, you take her upstairs and show her one of the people we rescued. The following day

Captain Johnson marches into the house, accompanied by seven men with muskets, and you say it has nothing to do with her?"

"In case you had forgotten, she saved me in there," said Oliver, his brow darkening. "If she hadn't spoken up for me they would have had an excuse to take me away, and I'd have been on my way to prison, or to Duchamp, at this very moment."

"That was nothing but a clever ruse, to throw you off the scent and make you trust her more."

"An unnecessary ruse. They had me in their power. Why would they need me to trust her after that?"

"Because Duchamp is playing a deep game, and trying to catch the people we rescue as well as catching us."

"Either that, or Captain Johnson is playing a game of his own," mused James. "He knows there's a reward on our heads, and having found out where we are, he could have decided to play for bigger stakes. There's a reward on the head of anyone we rescue as well. He could have sent Susannah here to befriend us. Then he arrives threatening to arrest you. She leaps to your defence in the hope that you'll take her further into your confidence and tell her the time of the next landing. Then she can let Captain Johnson know so that he can be there to intercept us. He will not only claim the reward on our heads, if that's the case, but a dozen or more extra rewards as well."

"No," said Oliver, banging the table with his fist. "You're wrong. She doesn't have anything to do with the militia. She can't have. She hasn't left the house since I was attacked, and if this plan you're imagining had been in place by then, I wouldn't have been attacked in the first place."

"She could have left last night without you knowing about it," returned Edward.

"No, she couldn't. I locked the doors."

"She has keys."

"Had keys."

"What do you mean?" asked Edward, his brows drawing together. "Do you mean you took them?"

James and Edward looked at him.

Oliver's eyes glinted. "It seemed like a wise precaution at the time."

"Then you don't trust her," said Edward thoughtfully.

"I didn't. I do now."

"She didn't need to leave." It was James who spoke.

Edward glanced at him. "What do you mean?"

"She could have passed a note to the boy. The one who brings the milk in the mornings. She gives him letters. I've seen her do it. She could easily have passed him a message for the captain, and had a message in return the same way. She and Captain Johnson could have planned this when she found out how close she was getting to you," he said to Oliver.

"I don't believe it," said Oliver, jumping up and striding across the room. "She wouldn't do something like that. I know it."

"Perhaps you're right," conceded Edward. "Miss Thorpe could be innocent. She could be exactly who she says she is, and the scene we have just witnessed could have been genuine, but there is a spy here somewhere, someone who alerted Duchamp's agents to our presence. If it isn't Miss Thorpe, it could be one of the villagers. It could be Tregornan. Or it could be the boy. He could have been chosen specifically for the job here."

James's eyes widened. "It's possible. I was talking to Kelsey once—we were discussing a sailing—and I noticed that Jim stopped whistling as he crossed the yard behind us."

"You think he was listening?"

"He could have been."

"Hm." Edward drummed his fingers on the table. "There's no way to be sure. But we've had two brushes with the militia, and it won't stop there. Captain Johnson means to claim the reward, and he won't be satisifed until he's done it. He's holding back at the moment. My guess is that he's decided to try and catch more fish in his net, but he won't hold back for ever. We must make sure we don't talk in front of the boy again, and we must keep away from the village. We can't help Tregornan knowing the times of our sailings, but if you've any sense," he went on, turning to Oliver, "you won't talk in front of Miss Thorpe either."

"She'll know where we've gone the next time we leave the house," Oliver pointed out.

"But not when we'll be back, and without that knowledge the captain can't catch us as we come ashore."

"What do we do if he returns?" asked James.

"We just have to hope he doesn't, at least not until it's too late. We have time to make one more sailing, and after that our work here will be done."

CHAPTER TEN

Susannah was worried about Oliver. He was going to France again, and the militia were on the alert. It would be an easy matter for one of them to kill him and then declare it was in the line of duty, and she could only hope that the soldiers did not discover the time of his next rescue mission.

She busied herself with her inventory of the house and drew a plan for each of the sitting-rooms in the west wing, deciding how she wanted to furnish them. She was aided in this by another letter from Mrs. Wise, which enclosed engravings of furniture taken from *Ackermann's Repository*.

It was whilst she was engaged in these plans that there was once again a knock at the door, and her heart began to pound as she feared that the militia had returned. But instead, when Susannah opened the door, she saw that a well-dressed lady stood there with her two daughters.

"Miss Thorpe?" said the lady in a friendly fashion, looking Susannah up and down.

She had dark brown hair and brown eyes.

"Yes," said Susannah, a trifle warily.

"I am Mrs. Trevennan, your new neighbour. Forgive me for not leaving a card, but here in the country we are more friendly than people in town and we pay our visits without quite so much formality," she said with a smile. "Neighbour needs neighbour here, particularly in the winter, and as soon as I found out you were in residence I knew I should pay a call."

"That's very kind of you," said Susannah. She opened the door wide, and was so relieved they were not the militia that she made them doubly welcome. "Do, please, come in. I hope you will excuse me answering the door myself," she went on, as they entered the hall. "I have not yet had time to appoint a household staff."

"I quite understand. We have not come to criticize, but to make you welcome, have we not, girls?"

The two Miss Trevennans giggled and nodded their heads.

They had dark hair like their mother, and the same bright eyes. They wore matching blue coats, and wore adorable hats over an abundance of ringlets which cascaded down their backs. They were, perhaps, sixteen and seventeen years old, thought Susannah, clearly out of the schoolroom, but without the social poise that came with experience of society. They looked ready to giggle and nod at anything their mother said.

"This is a charming house," said Mrs. Trevennan, as she followed Susannah into the sitting-room. "I have often said that it has one of the finest positions in Cornwall, and it was a shame it has stood empty for so long. But now you are here, it has a mistress again. You will find yourself very popular, Miss Thorpe. It's a long time since we had new blood in the neighbourhood, and you will be a welcome addition to our society. Is that not so, girls?"

The two Miss Trevennans giggled.

"Please, take a seat," said Susannah.

Mrs. Trevennan arranged her exquisite cloak around her and sat on the sofa, laying her fur muff by her side.

"Have you lived in Cornwall long?" asked Susannah.

"There have been Trevennans here for hundreds of years," said Mrs. Trevennan. "Our house is just around the headland, not five miles away. It is a pleasant walk in the summer. We do so hope you mean to settle here, and that you don't mean to spend your life in town?"

"I have not quite decided yet," said Susannah.

"I must not bully you. We can but hope," she said with a smile. "You must come and see us when you have settled in. We cannot offer you much by way of entertainment at the moment, but at Christmas, Robert will be home. Robert is my son," she said to Susannah, beaming proudly. "He is such a handsome boy! I think I may say, without any of a mother's partiality, that he is the finest man hereabouts, and, of course, he is his father's heir. He will have Trevennan House and all the land around it. Although our two houses are five miles apart, the estates border each other, you know."

"How nice," said Susannah politely.

She was beginning to think that Mrs. Trevennan had an ulterior motive for her visit. It seemed that news of her arrival and inheritance had spread, and Mrs. Trevennan was clearly viewing her as a possible daughter-in-law. But it was not to be wondered at. Heiresses were the rightful property of impecunious landowners, or, at least, so most mothers of impecunious landowners thought!

It told her one thing, though, thought Susannah. News of her supposed engagement had not spread, otherwise Mrs. Trevennan would not have been so eager to call. It was some consolation. At least when Oliver left, she would not have to explain the circumstance to her neighbours.

Mrs. Trevennan turned out to be a wise woman. Having introduced her son into the conversation, she said no more of him. Instead she talked of the weather, the problems of smoking chimneys, and the latest fashions, before bringing her visit to an end.

"We must not leave the horses too long," she explained, when the time allotted for a formal visit had elapsed. "John is walking them, but he will scold me if I keep him waiting any longer. I declare, Miss Thorpe, I am a slave to my coachman!" She rose to her feet. "It has been a pleasure to meet you."

"And you. It was good of you to call."

"Now don't forget, we are relying on you to take dinner with us when Roderick comes home," said Mrs. Trevennan, as Susannah showed her and her daughters to the door. "He will be so disappointed if he does not have a chance to meet you."

Roderick? thought Susannah with a sudden chill. But aloud, she said, "Thank you, you are very kind."

"Nonsense! What are neighbours for? If you need any help or advice, then I hope you will send a message to me. I will enjoy nothing more than putting you in the way of the best shopkeepers or advising you on the most reliable farrier."

Susannah thanked her again, and the Trevennans departed, climbing into their smartly appointed carriage. The coachman closed the door behind them, mounted his box and cracked the whip, then the carriage rolled away down the drive.

As Susannah closed the door, she leant back against it, thinking. To begin with, Mrs. Trevennan's visit had seemed like nothing more than the natural curiosity of near neighbours, but now she wasn't so sure, and she felt she needed someone to talk to. Constance would know no more than she did, but she would value Oliver's advice.

She went upstairs, knowing he was to take his turn sitting with Buvoir that morning. She scratched softly at the door, and a voice called, "Come in."

It was not Oliver's voice, however, but Kelsey's.

"I thought I would find Mr. Bristow here," Susannah said, as she went into the room.

"He's gone down to the shore," Kelsey said.

"I see. Thank you."

She was about to leave, when she saw that Buvoir was out of bed. He was sitting by the window, fully dressed, reading a book.

"I see you are feeling better," she said.

He looked up with a smile, but it was clear he had not understood her.

Her French was limited, but she managed to ask after his health and learnt that he was much recovered, and that he would soon be leaving to stay with friends in the north-east.

Leaving Kelsey with Buvoir, she went to her own room and changed, then went downstairs. She breathed in deeply as she stepped out into the fine morning. The sky was blue and the wind had dropped, giving a clear, sunny day. She had never seen the landscape look so vibrant. The grass was emerald, and the sea was a sparkling sapphire. Glints of sunlight winked from the water, bringing it to life. She turned her steps towards the edge of the cliff and soon came to the path. She scrambled down. There was no sign of Oliver in the first cove, but as she rounded the shore she saw him at the jetty of boulders, just about to untie the rowing boat. She hurried along the jetty to greet him.

"Susannah!" he said, looking up at her approach. "Is anything wrong?"

"Perhaps. I don't know," she said with a frown.

He glanced from her to the boat.

"Would you care to go out?"

"In the rowing boat?" she asked.

"Yes."

"I thought the currents were deadly," she remarked humorously.

He laughed. "It is your curiosity that could have been deadly. The currents are safe enough, as long as they are treated with respect."

"Then yes, thank you, I would," she said.

He held out his hand to her.

She hesitated for a fraction of a second, then took it. Even through her glove she could feel the contact, and she avoided looking into his face. He would soon be leaving, and she had no business giving in to instincts that led her beyond the bounds of propriety. Instead she looked at the boat, judging its rhythm as it bobbed into the jetty and away again. Waiting until it had gone to its furthest point she lifted her foot, and by the time she brought her foot down, the boat had bobbed to shore once again. She stepped in, wobbled precariously until she had brought her other foot into the boat, and then sat down facing Oliver.

He untied the boat and pushed it away from the jetty with an oar, then began to row. Once he had taken them clear of the cove, he said, "What's troubling you?"

"It might be nothing," she said, "but I've just had a visit from one of my neighbours, a Mrs. Trevennan."

"Yes?"

"I thought to begin with, it was nothing more than friendliness, combined with a desire to secure an heiress for her son, but now I'm not so sure. She told me that her son, Robert, would be coming home at Christmas and invited me to dine with them when he is here. We went on to talk of other things, but as she was leaving she reminded me of the invitation. Only this time, she called her son Roderick."

He was thoughtful.

"So you don't think she's a neighbour," he said.

"Yes, I do," said Susannah, considering. "She told me where she lived and invited me to call on her, so I believe she lives there, but not that she came for a neighbourly purpose."

"You think she was sent to spy on you?"

"Or perhaps to find out if my engagement to you was real. She made no mention of it, and I thought it was because the captain had not told anyone, but by talking about her imaginery son she could have been wanting me to say that I was already betrothed."

"Then the good captain didn't believe us, and he has persuaded one of the local gentry to discover the truth. Goodness knows what inducement he used," he said with a frown, as he pulled on the oars. "Perhaps he is willing to overlook her husband's use of smuggled brandy if she helps him in this matter."

"I suspected as much," said Susannah. "There was something in the captain's face when he left that told me he hadn't accepted the story, but there was nothing he could say. I think you're right. He wants to know the truth."

"Then we had better be prepared for more visits from Captain Johnson," said Oliver.

They fell silent.

At last, Susannah said, "Do you think I'll have any more calls from the Trevennans?"

"You might do. It's as well to be on your guard."

"Shall I tell them that we are engaged, if they wait on me?" she asked.

He thought. "I think not, unless they ask you directly. That will keep the captain guessing. He's not yet sure I'm the man he wants. With any luck, by the time he is sure, we'll be gone."

Susannah's spirits dropped. The sky was as blue as ever, and the sun as warm, but the pleasure had gone out of her day.

"Where will you go when you leave Harstairs House?" she asked.

She tried to make her voice sound unconcerned, but it came out on a drooping note.

He rested on the oars and looked at her, his expression softening.

"Somewhere else along the coast. Far enough away from here to be unknown. Then we can carry on with our work."

"And what will happen to the people you save? Where will they go?"

"To safe houses. Some people have relatives or friends in the country, in which case we take them there. Others are not so fortunate, and they are taken in by those who sympathize with their plight."

She shivered.

"It's such a short distance across the Channel, and yet there is more than water separating us. Our lives here go on as before; theirs are in turmoil."

And whilst they were, Oliver would go on putting himself in danger, she thought.

"How much longer will it last?" she asked.

"I don't know. I had hoped it would be over by now. When the king was murdered I thought it couldn't get any worse, but I was wrong. It was only just beginning." He rested on the oars and looked out to sea. The waves gently rocked the boat, and their regular lapping was the only sound.

"There must come an end sometime," said Susannah. "It cannot go on for ever."

"Eventually, it will burn itself out," he agreed. "Until then, I must do what I can to help those trapped in its clutches. But this is a sad topic for such a beautiful day," he went on, picking up the oars again. "Let us be thankful we live on this side of the Channel, and that we can enjoy it."

Susannah responded to his smile and felt her feelings grow. As the boat sculled over the waves, she delighted in the feel of the sun on her face and the sound of the gulls above her. It was difficult to believe that there was anything but beauty in the world. As a breeze rose, and blew exhilaratingly in her face, she raised her hand to her hat to keep it from blowing away, but it was too late. A sudden gust of wind whipped it away and blew it over the sea. It skipped along the waves before settling some little distance away.

"Oh, no!" she cried.

He laughed, and she shared his laughter. He turned the boat and rowed with strong, powerful strokes towards it. Then, shipping the oars, he lifted it out of the water before it became waterlogged and sank.

"Thank you!" she said, as he returned it to her.

His hand touched hers, and she looked into his eyes. Here was a man who risked his life saving innocents from the revolution, and yet he could still laugh and take a delight in life. As her heart turned over inside her, she knew it was not just admiration or respect she felt for him, it was love.

"We should be going back," he said.

She nodded. It would do her no good to encourage her feelings. He was to leave Harstairs House soon, and he had never spoken of having any feelings for her. He was a man of action, not a man who would settle down and take a wife. She should feel betrayed that he had kissed her without intending to ask for her hand, or humiliated, or spurned, but she felt none of those things. Instead she felt only thankfulness that he had come into her life.

He turned the boat and rowed them back to the shore. Shipping the oars, he sprang out on to the jetty, taking the rope with him. He tied the boat fast then offered her his hand and helped her out. They stood for a moment looking at each other, then he turned towards the path and she fell into step beside him. They did not talk on the way back, but once they reached the house, he said to her, "Susannah?"

"Yes?" she asked, turning to face him.

"When I told Captain Johnson we were betrothed . . ."

"Yes?" she asked breathlessly.

"I would like it very much if–"

"You're back."

Edward's harsh voice broke in on them and the moment shattered like glass.

Oliver exhaled sharply.

"Yes," he said. "I am."

"Good. I need to speak to you. When you're ready," he added, with a touch of sarcasm in his voice.

"Very well."

Oliver made her a bow and left her.

Susannah, glancing after him, saw Edward's uncompromising face.

He doesn't trust me, she thought. *He thinks I have betrayed them.*

~   ~   ~

"Well?" asked Oliver, as he followed Edward into the library.

Edward sat down and rested his elbows on the table. "I think we should put our next trip to France forward by a few days."

Oliver swept up the tails of his coat and sat down opposite him. "Because?" he demanded.

"Because the sooner we finish our work here and leave, the better," said Edward impatiently.

Oliver shook his head. "Our plans are already made. We can't change everything now. Tregornan knows when to have the ship ready for us. It's all arranged."

"It will be safer," said Edward. "News of our plans might have leaked out."

"No," said Oliver.

"You seem to think it's your decision alone." Edward's mouth was a tight line in his face.

"It is. I'm grateful for everything you and James have done, but this has been my affair from the beginning. I've organized the trips, I've paid for ships, I've found our bases—everything has been of my doing. If you don't like that, then I'm sorry, but it's not about to change now." His expression relented. "Don't worry. This is our last trip from this house. It will be all right. We have to risk it."

"Very well." Edward stood up. "But I warn you, Oliver, if you behave as obtusely in the future as you've done over the last few weeks, you and I will part company."

"If that's the way it has to be," said Oliver.

"As long as we know where we both stand."

Oliver nodded curtly, and Edward left the room.

A few weeks before, Oliver thought, he would have

agreed with Edward: speaking to anyone outside their small group about their missions was dangerous, and could compromise their security. But now everything had changed. He smiled as he thought of it. He didn't regret telling Susannah about what he was doing. He loved her. He trusted her. In the hall, he had almost asked her to be his wife, and the thought of marrying her filled him with joy. Not long ago, he had decided he must give her up, but now he knew he couldn't do it.

Going over to the window, he looked out over the ocean. Until recently, rescuing the helpless from the clutches of the revolution had been the most important thing in his life, but it paled beside his love for Susannah. But he couldn't risk leaving her a widow, that much had not changed, and so his dangerous exploits must come to an end. He had one final mission to complete, but when it was over he knew that his future lay with Susannah, and that he would go to France no more.

CHAPTER ELEVEN

"A letter has arrived," said Constance, as Susannah went into the kitchen a week later. Constance wiped her hands on her apron and then took the letter down from the mantelpiece. "Jim brought it this morning. I meant to give it to you before now, but I forgot."

Susannah took the proffered letter and opened it.

"It's from Mr. Sinders," she said, pulling a chair up to the fire. "He has made enquiries about Jim's family and found them to be satisfactory. He had already met Jim before entrusting the lad with the task of bringing the milk, and although he considered him impertinent, he also considered him eager and trustworthy. He knows nothing against any of the family, except that one of the brothers drinks, but as I am not thinking of employing him it does not signify."

"Then we will be appointing Jim's sisters?"

"We will."

"Good," said Constance in relief. "The wash house is almost full to overflowing."

Susannah returned the letter to the mantelpiece and went into the wash house to have a look for herself. There were sheets, towels and patchwork quilts to be mended. There were rugs and curtains to be beaten. The whole room was a jumble of colourful confusion.

"I will hire them as soon as I am sure of my inheritance," said Susannah. "I only hope we get a spell of dry weather. It will be impossible to dry anything if this rain lasts."

"It won't, or at least so Jim tells me," said Constance. "He's consulted the seaweed or some such thing. He's promised to show me how to do it, so that I can foretell the weather on washing days."

"If it works, it will be a miracle!" laughed Susannah.

"Anything that helps me avoid a hedgeful of wet washing in a downpour is worth trying," said Constance.

Susannah agreed. She had spent many wash days with Aunt Caroline, running in and out of the house with armfuls of washing, bringing it in even wetter than when she had put it out.

"We haven't seen much of the gentlemen recently," said Constance, as she stoked the fire. "I usually see them going to or from the stables, or perhaps bump into them in the hall, but they seem to be keeping themselves to themselves."

"I dare say they are busy," said Susannah.

In fact, the gentlemen had gone to France. She had seen Oliver only once since their afternoon's boating, and learnt of his last mission. He had been facing terrible dangers for days whilst she had gone quietly about her keeping house. But it would do no good to dwell on it. They meant to return on the evening tide, and she must occupy her mind until they were safely within the walls of Harstairs House once more.

She was grateful for one thing. Buvoir had recovered sufficiently to be moved, and was no longer in the house. He was on his way to London, assisted by those who opposed the revolution, and from there he would go to a friend's house, where he would begin a new life.

"I think I will look over the kitchen garden," she said. "Once I employ Jim's father, I will need to tell him what I want to do with it. We must grow vegetables and herbs, but I would like to try and grow a few flowers, too."

"Oh, yes, that would be lovely," said Constance. "There is nothing like the scent of flowers in the summer, and some bright colours to gladden the eye."

Susannah went outside, but she found it difficult to concentrate. She made a few desultory plans for planting vegetables, and wondered if it was warm enough for peaches to grow against the house wall, but her thoughts were with Oliver. He would be home soon, she thought, looking out to sea. The short winter afternoon was passing, and already she could make out very little. In another half-hour darkness would fall, the tide would turn, and he would come back again.

She turned her attention back to the garden, and was just deciding it would be sensible to put a path down the centre of the patch to make it easier to weed when Constance joined her. One look at Constance's face showed her that something was wrong.

"What is it?" she asked.

"It's the militia. They're here again. I didn't want to disturb you when I heard someone at the door, in case it was just a neighbour leaving a card, but it was Captain Johnson. He asked to see you. I told him you were busy. I don't approve of soldiers forcing their way into decent homes and accusing people of things they haven't done," she said. "I was about to close the door when he put his boot in the way and asked for Mr. Bristow. I told him Mr. Bristow was out and tried to close the door again, but somehow he managed to push it open and walked inside. He was very polite, but I don't trust him. He wasn't invited in, and yet he came in anyway. He said he needed to see Mr. Bristow and that he would wait. I tried to show him into the sitting-room, but he took himself into the library instead, though how he knew where it was is beyond me. He has settled himself down there, and says he will stay there until Mr. Bristow's return."

Susannah's face registered her alarm, and Constance said, "I'm sorry, I never meant to let him in."

"It's not your fault," said Susannah, plucking at her cloak.

"I hope there's nothing wrong?" asked Constance.

Susannah wondered what to say, but decided she must take Constance into her confidence.

"I'm afraid to say that something is very much wrong. I have not been honest with you Constance, and I hope you will forgive me, but it was done for the best. Mr. Bristow and his friends are not here to try and find an estate to buy, they are here to rescue people from France. That is why they took Harstairs House. They needed somewhere on the coast, so that they could put out to sea without being seen."

"Oh my!" When Constance had recovered from her shock, she said, "I had no idea. What a brave thing to do—and what a dangerous one." Her brow furrowed. "But I don't see what it has to do with the militia."

"Some of the militia are hoping to claim a reward offered by a Jacobin named Duchamp, who wants to stop anyone attempting to run rescue missions. He has put a price on Oliver's head."

Constance paled.

"What are we to do?" she said.

"We must try and lure the militia out of the library. There is a secret passage there, leading up from the cove. Somehow, Captain Johnson must have learnt of it, as he must have learnt that Oliver is due to return tonight, which is why he is sitting there. He means to catch Oliver as he emerges from the passage with the men and women he has rescued. The captain is hoping to claim a reward for Oliver and his friends, and for every escaped prisoner they have saved."

"But how are we to do it?" asked Constance.

Susannah's spirits fell. She did not see any way of forcing armed men to leave a room they had chosen to sit in.

"I confess, I can't see a way, so we must think of something else. I know. I will go down to the beach and warn Oliver. He will be landing soon. I will tell him not to come up to the house. He will have to wait in one of the coves until the militia have departed."

"Oh, no, that won't do," said Constance, shaking her head.

"Why not?" asked Susannah.

"Because Captain Johnson said that if Mr. Bristow had gone down to the beach, he would meet his men. They were patrolling the shore, he said, as there were smugglers in the neighbourhood."

"They mean to cut him off," said Susannah. "They must know where the other end of the secret passage lies. They will wait for him to go into the cave and then guard the exit. If he tries to double back once he knows the captain is in the library, he will be caught."

"Whatever are we to do?" asked Constance anxiously.

An idea was already forming at the back of Susannah's mind.

"There is another passage," she said. "It's under the sundial in the courtyard garden. I discovered it when I was cleaning and pressed the 'o' of the sundial's motto: 'Time and tide wait for no man.' I don't know exactly where it leads, but when I opened it I heard the sea, so it must lead to somewhere along the beach. I mean to follow it, and then use it to provide Oliver with a safe route to the house."

"I'll come with you," said Constance stoutly.

"No. I need you to stay here and keep an eye on the militia. Don't let them go into the courtyard garden. I dare not pull the sundial back in place after myself in case I become trapped. It should not be obvious that it has been moved unless the captain goes into the courtyard, and I see no reason why he should do that. Try and keep them from leaving the library. As long as they are there, we know where they are."

"But if they want to explore, how will I stop them?" asked Constance.

"I'm sure you'll think of a way," said Susannah, putting her hand on Constance's shoulder.

"I will do my best. But won't you be afraid in the dark?" asked Constance. "The light's fading fast, and it will be black in the passage."

"I'll take the storm lantern. My only worry is what we can do with the people Oliver has rescued once we get them back to the house. Some of them may be injured. They will all be cold and probably wet. There will be women and children amongst them," she said, as she went into the kitchen. "We will need somewhere to hide them until the militia depart."

"The fire's lit in the sitting-room," said Constance. "We can take them in there."

"But will the sitting-room be safe? I don't think so. When Oliver doesn't return, the captain might grow impatient and search the house."

"We can put them in the attic," said Constance. "There's plenty of room up there."

"But the stairs creak dreadfully. We could get one or two people up the stairs, perhaps, if we were lucky, but not more. We would be heard."

She stopped, her eyes on the far wall.

"What is it?" asked Constance, following her gaze.

"The wash house," said Susannah with energy. "If we hide them in there, then once they are inside, we can push the dresser in front of the door. It will completely cover it, and the captain will not even know it is there. There is no other entrance. It will be as if the room does not exist."

"It will be cold in there," said Constance consideringly. "I'd better light a fire."

"Do that, and put the rugs down on the floor." She gave a faint smile. "It's fortunate we carried so many towels and quilts in there. At least the rescued people will be able to dry themselves and keep themselves warm. Have the kettle boiling so we can give everyone a hot drink when they arrive, and put some food in the wash house. Once we have covered the door we want to make sure it can remain closed overnight if necessary. You had better put some whisky in there, too. Remember, they will have spent hours on a ship."

"I'll see to everything," said Constance, adding under her breath, "including chamber pots."

"Good. Then I must go. If the captain asks after me, tell him I have gone for a walk."

"Very good."

She picked up the storm lantern, then hurried upstairs to the sitting-room, moving as quietly as she could. Her heart was beating rapidly by the time she reached it, as she had feared that at any moment Captain Johnson might come out of the library and see her. But she managed to gain the room without mishap.

She lit the candle at the fire and closed the glass sides of the lantern, then she went into the courtyard. She put the lantern down beside the sundial, then pushed the centre of the 'o' and the dial swung aside. She felt a surge of fear as she looked down into the black hole, but reminding herself that she was Oliver's only hope she steeled her nerve and set her foot on the first step. It was slimy, and her foot almost slipped away from under her. It would be easier in bare feet. Sitting down on the rim of the hole, she removed her boots and stockings, then placing them carefully on the top step she tried again. The step was cold and wet, but her grip was much more secure. Picking up the lantern, she moved down to the next step, balancing herself with one hand against the wall.

It's like being a child again, she thought, as she descended carefully. She remembered all the times she had clambered over wet rocks as a little girl, leaving her shoes and stockings on the beach. If she had had a nursemaid she would not have been allowed to do such a thing, but her father had seen nothing wrong with it and she had enjoyed many hours of such freedom. It was standing her in good stead now.

There was no light but candlelight to guide her. The fading daylight from the hole above her had completely disappeared. She had the stone wall on her right side, a steep drop to her left, and the steps at her feet. She fixed her eyes firmly on the next step, going down slowly and cautiously and making sure she had a firm footing before she trusted her weight to the next step. It was cold underfoot. The sound of the sea grew louder, and her heart began to beat more quickly. She knew nothing about the passage, or where it came out. What if it came out into a cave that was flooded at high tide? She might not be able to get down to the beach. Even worse, she might get down and not be able to get back. Or what if it flooded whilst she was in it, and if the water came in so quickly she was drowned?

Resolutely she pushed those thoughts aside. It could not be helped. She had to warn Oliver, and this was the only way. She must just move as quickly as possible, and hope for the best.

She descended more rapidly now. She had grown accustomed to the feel of the weed beneath her feet, and she moved with a sure footing. Every now and then she stepped on a sharp piece of rock and winced, but she still kept going down. Here and there she came across a landing where she could stop and catch her breath, but she did not want to. She was all too aware of the sound of the sea, which was coming nearer and nearer.

At last she reached the bottom of the steps and found herself in a cave. It was much smaller than the cave she had entered from the passage in the library. It had no sandy bottom, but instead it was lined with boulders, between which the sea was churning. The water looked cold, and she shivered. If she fell in . . . the pools seemed bottomless, and they had such steep sides she doubted if she would ever be able to climb out.

Keeping to the edge of the cave, she made her way to the light that filtered in dimly from somewhere ahead of her. The noise of the surf became louder, until at last she found herself on the coast. The cave was fronted by rocks, but the sea had not yet reached its mouth, and she realized that the water in the cave pools must remain there constantly, instead of filling and emptying with the tide. She looked to left and right, trying to get her bearings, and was relieved to recognize a rock not far to her right. She had seen it when she and Oliver had gone out in the boat. It was about the height of a man, with a bulbous bottom and a sharp, pointed spike on top. If she walked round it she would find herself in the cove with the jetty.

Moving cautiously, aware of the fact that she could run into soldiers at any minute, she rounded the rock. There ahead of her was the sandy cove, and nearing it was a longboat. Two men were pulling on the oars—Edward and Oliver! There was a group of other people in the boat with them. She recognized James and Kelsey, and saw that there were about twenty people besides. Some were men but most were women, and there appeared to be a few children amongst them.

The boat pulled into the jetty and Oliver leapt out.

"What are you doing here?" he demanded. "Don't you know the danger you're in? You—"

"There are soldiers here," she interrupted him. "They're at the house, sitting and waiting for you in the library."

He cursed. "Then we must hide in the cave."

"No. There are soldiers on the shore as well."

"Whereabouts?" he asked, looking round.

"I don't know. I haven't seen them. They might not have arrived yet. They were coming from the house. But they're on their way, if they're not here already, and they are likely to search the caves."

Oliver's voice was grim. "Then they've cut us off. Unless . . . if they've not yet reached the top of the cliff path, perhaps we can reach it before them. If so, we might be able to slip past them and escape into the countryside," he said, scanning the cliffs.

"There's another way, another passage," she said. "It goes up to the courtyard garden that leads off from the sitting-room. Quickly. Follow me."

Without wasting time asking questions he nodded curtly, and as the tired men, women and children climbed wearily out of the longboat, he directed them to follow Susannah.

She retraced her steps back along the shore towards the rock. As she rounded it she looked back to see Oliver helping the last few people out of the boat, and then heard him softly wish the men who remained in the longboat God speed. She saw them begin to row out again and glanced out to sea, noticing the dim outline of a ship anchored some way out. Then she turned her attention back to the rocks.

The tide was now nearer the cave mouth than it had been. It was creeping closer, and she was worried they would not all reach the cave in time. Some of the people were injured. They were all very tired. She led the way, holding the storm lantern aloft, and doing what she could to encourage everyone following her to make haste. Once at the cave mouth she stopped to make sure the others were behind her. They were. She was just about to turn and go in when she heard a loud crack! tear into the night. It was the sound of a musket being fired.

Oliver! she thought.

"Go on!" came Oliver's voice from somewhere behind her.

Knowing she must not dally, she said, "Be careful. Keep close to the wall. The rocks are slippery and there are deep pools to your right."

Having warned them, she went into the cave. As quickly as she could, she crossed the rocks, using one hand to steady herself against the wall to her left, whilst holding the lantern aloft with her right. She had gone about halfway when she felt something cold wash over her feet. It was the sea.

Spurred on by the rising tide, she quickened her pace as

she headed towards the steps at the back of the cave, then breathed a sigh of relief as she reached them and started to ascend. She came to the first landing and was about to turn and go up again when she heard a cry and a splash. There was the sound of a child's whimpering, and James's voice saying, "Damn!" from the darkness. Then Oliver's voice called, "Carry on!"

There was nothing she could do to help. She turned and went upwards.

Up, up, she went, as the sound of the rushing tide grew louder in her ears. It was pouring into the cave. She reached the last few steps . . . and almost hit her head on solid stone. The sundial had swung shut. She felt her heart begin to pound. They were trapped!

CHAPTER TWELVE

How had it happened? She knew the dial would swing shut of its own accord if it was half closed, but she had left it wide open. Had the captain found it? Had he searched the house and shut them in? She looked down, and saw the water rising. If they didn't get out, they would be drowned. She began fumbling on the wall, hoping she could find a catch that would move the sundial out of the way.

"Here, hold this," she said.

She thrust the lantern into the hands of the woman on the step below her so that she could use both hands to search. She felt all along the roof, trying to find some hole or lever, but she found nothing.

"Don't stop!" came Oliver's voice from below. "Go up!"

"I can't," she called back, trying to keep the panic out of her voice. "The hole has closed."

"What?!"

There was movement on the steps below her. The ragged Frenchmen and women huddled to one side as Oliver pushed past them, until he stood two steps below Susannah.

"There's a sundial covering the hole," she said quickly. "I left it open, but someone must have closed it."

"There must be a catch," he said, feeling the roof and walls.

"I thought so, too, but I can't find one."

There was more disturbance below them, and Edward joined them.

"Set your shoulder to it," he said to Oliver.

Oliver put his shoulder to the roof. Susannah descended a few steps so that Edward could do the same. They heaved, trying to push the heavy dial to the side, but it would not move. At last, panting heavily with the exertion, they stopped to rest.

"Which way does it go?" asked Oliver.

Susannah thought. "To the left," she said.

They tried again, to no avail.

"The water's on the bottom step," James called up from below. "It's rising quickly."

"Caught like rats in a trap," said Edward grimly.

"We're not finished yet," said Oliver. "James! We need you and Kelsey up here!"

There came the sound of feet slapping on wet rock and then James joined them.

"Where's Kelsey?" asked Edward.

"I don't know. I haven't seen him since we got out of the boat."

"He rounded the rock," said Oliver.

"Then where is he? Oh, no," said James, his voice sinking. "The musket shot. It must have hit him."

There was silence as they took it in. Then Edward spoke. "If he's gone, he's gone. Right now, we need to get out of here, or we'll all be joining him."

Susannah retreated further down the steps, leaving the three men to try and heave the dial aside, but it would not move.

Oliver looked down into the water, which was still rising.

"We'll have to swim for it," he said, as he took his shoulder from the roof.

"We could perhaps manage it, as long as the tide does not come in too quickly and does not reach the roof, but the émigrés will never manage it," said James in a low voice. "There are children amongst them, and some of the men and women are too weak to make the effort."

"There's no other way," Edward said. "We–"

And then there was a grating sound, and the roof above them began to move. A dim light filtered in, and gradually became brighter as moonlight shone into the passage. It was accompanied by the blessed smell of fresh air.

"How . . . ?" began James.

"Never mind that now. Get everyone out."

Oliver sprang up the last few steps and leapt out, turning to help the others. One by one he half pulled, half lifted them out. Susannah was first.

"Oh, I'm so glad you're all right," came Constance's voice from out of the shadows. "I've been so worried."

"Constance! What are you doing here?"

"The militia began searching the house, and the captain told them to make sure they searched the courtyard garden, too. I had to slip outside and shut the passage in case they discovered it. I was afraid you would be drowned, but I couldn't open it again until they went upstairs. Thank goodness you're safe. But come, quickly. The soldiers are in the attic now, those that aren't in the library. You have time to get everyone into the kitchen."

Susannah and Constance led the way across the courtyard, through the french doors, over the corridor and down the steps into the kitchen. Susannah breathed a sigh of relief as she stepped into the light. Never had the kitchen seemed more welcoming. The kettle was steaming over the fire, and the room was bathed in a yellow glow. But she had no

AMANDA GRANGE

time to revel in its homeliness. She set the lantern down on the mantelpiece and turned round to see a raggedly dressed line of people following her.

Three women came first, with a girl of about eight years of age, then came an old man with a dirtily bandaged head wound and after him came two young men. James followed them into the kitchen carrying a boy of about five years old. He was wet through, and Susannah guessed he must have fallen into the rock pool. An assortment of seventeen people passed into the kitchen, together with Oliver, James and Edward, before Oliver closed the door behind them.

"Into the wash house," said Susannah, leading the way.

A large fire was burning brightly. A kettle was set over it, and assorted cups and dishes were placed next to it. Constance began pouring out dishes of hot tea and lacing them with whisky, handing them to the adults as they came through the door. The children were given hot milk.

"They can't stay here," said Oliver. "If the militia are searching the house, it's only a matter of time before they come downstairs. We have to get everyone out to the stables, and hope that we can get at least some of them away."

"There's no need," said Susannah, untying the strings of her cloak and slipping it from her shoulders. "As soon as the militia make a move towards the kitchen, we can push the dresser across the door. It will obscure it entirely.

234

There is no other entrance. The wash house will simply disappear."

He looked at her with a mixture of admiration and respect, and a smile crossed his face.

"We'll outwit them yet!" he said.

"Constance," said Susannah, "go to the top of the steps and let us know as soon as the militia start to come this way."

Constance handed out a final dish of tea, then left the kitchen, closing the door behind her.

"James, Edward, help me," said Oliver.

The three men went into the kitchen and pushed the dresser across the door, leaving only a small gap. It was big enough for one person to slip through so that they could go in and out until the last minute if needed.

"We won't push it fully across until we have to," he said.

Susannah nodded. She glanced upwards at the clothes airer suspended from the ceiling. She unwrapped the cord from the hook on the wall and lowered the airer, then hung a sheet over it. She raised it part way to the ceiling, so that the sheet just skimmed the floor. It provided a screen separating the two sides of the room. Encouraging the men into one side and the women and children into the other, she began to hand out towels so that they could dry themselves, then turned her attention to the boy who had fallen in the pool.

"Where are his parents?" she asked.

"Dead," said Oliver, his mouth grim. "We tried to save them, but we were too late."

Susannah felt a lump in her throat, but crying would not help the boy now. He needed practical aid. Carrying him into the women's side of the room she undressed him and dried him thoroughly, wrapping him in a clean, dry sheet and then in a quilt. One of the women who had already dried herself held out her arms to the boy, crooning to him softly in French as he snuggled on to her knee.

"We will take care of him, my husband and me," she said.

Susannah helped the rest of the women remove their wet garments. Once everyone was wrapped in warm, dry linen she took down the sheet, opening the room up again, and began to hand out bread and cheese. Then she poured out glasses of wine, making sure that everyone had something to eat and drink.

She saw Edward watching her and felt uncomfortable, knowing what he thought of her, but after a few minutes he came towards her and said, "I'm sorry I doubted you. We owe you a great debt. Without you, we would have been caught in the passage or the library and everyone here would have been returned to France to face the guillotine—either that or killed outright. And this . . ." He looked round the room, with its leaping fire and its hastily assembled provisions. "This is a stroke of genius."

"It's lucky we had plenty of linen in here for washing and mending," she said. "Constance and I have been sorting through it for weeks."

"You're a brave woman, Susannah," he said, "and you have my gratitude—and my respect. But I will say no more. Oliver will never forgive me if I monopolize you," he finished with a smile.

Susannah flushed.

"I think we should close the gap," said Oliver, coming up to them. "We won't need to go in and out again. Everyone is warmly wrapped, and has food and drink. There will be no more need to go into the kitchen."

Briefly, he explained to the rescued men and women what was proposed. They understood at once, and were content to remain in the closed room until morning. Susannah discreetly pointed out the chamber pots, and then Susannah, James, Edward and Oliver went into the kitchen. Edward and James pushed the dresser across the door, and it was as though it did not exist. The kitchen looked peaceful in the dancing firelight, as though the worst it had ever seen was a spoilt roast.

"And now we had better make ourselves known to the good captain," said Oliver.

"James and I will go out to the stables," said Edward. "Then you and Susannah can claim to have been riding, and we can say that we are seeing to the horses. It will give

us an excuse for being dirty. But you should clean yourselves before you go above."

Susannah, who had caught sight of her reflection in the
window pane, could not have agreed more. Her cloak had
protected her gown from the dirt in the passage, but her
hair was wild, and her feet were bare. Worse still, she had
forgotten all about her shoes and stockings, and had left
them on the top step of the passage. They were still there,
or, even worse, they had been knocked into the sea.

Edward and James went out into the yard. Susannah
poured out a bowl of water and began to wash her face
and hands, whilst Oliver did the same. She turned her back
to him, but caught sight of his reflected naked torso in the
window as he stripped off his shirt and began to wash. She
stood, mesmerized, as she watched him. She had never
seen a man half naked before, and the sight of the water
running in rivulets over his lean, muscular form made her
pulse begin to race. She realized that she was staring and
looked away, but the memory lingered, and she wondered
how she was going to endure the pain of losing him when
he left.

She finished washing and then tidied her hair, taking it
down and running her fingers through it before piling it on
top of her head again. Glancing into the window pane, she
saw that Oliver had dressed himself once more, and she felt
free to turn round.

"We should go," he said. "I think it will be better if—"

His eyes fell to her feet.

"I took my boots and stockings off in the passage," she explained. "The steps were slippery, and I did not want to fall. It was easier to negotiate them in bare feet."

He smiled. "Riding with a man's saddle, bare-foot scrambling—it must have been an idyllic childhood. At least, I assume you learnt to scramble over rocks in your childhood?" he asked.

"Yes," she said with an answering smile. "Great Aunt Caroline would have been horrified if I had started to do it as an adult!"

His smile widened. Then his eye fell to her feet again.

"But you cannot go upstairs like that. Sit down."

"It's all right, I can manage," she protested.

He took no notice of her, but pushed her gently into a chair, then pouring a clean bowl of water he knelt before her, lifting her left foot on to his knee.

"So tiny," he murmured in wonder.

He took up a cloth and began tenderly washing her foot. As she felt the rhythmic stroke of the cloth on the sole of her foot she began to tingle, and an unnerving heat radiated outwards from every spot he touched. He washed away the caked sand, and then lowered her foot gently into the water, rubbing it with his long, strong fingers to dislodge the remaining specks of sand and lichen.

He lifted her other foot on to his knee and cleaned it equally gently. She began to tremble. She felt him stiffen, and looking down she saw that he would not raise his eyes to hers. She was not surprised. If he did, she knew that lightning would flash between them, the same lightning that had caught them in its grip when they had been riding on the cliff top. It threatened to consume them if a careless word or gesture summoned it, and she bit her lip in an effort to keep it at bay.

He took up a towel and dried her feet slowly, with great tenderness. Then he spread a towel on the floor and lifted her feet on to it.

"Susannah . . ." he said, at last looking up.

"Yes?" she asked, trembling at the look of longing on his face.

"Susannah, when I leave here . . ."

There came the sound of footsteps hurrying along the corridor, and Oliver turned away in frustration, cursing under his breath. A minute later the door opened, and Constance said, "The militia have finished searching the attic. They are making their report to the captain in the library, but once they have done so, I feel sure he will send men down here without delay."

Oliver rose quickly.

"Come, Susannah," he said. "It's time for us to fool the captain once again."

Susannah rose, then looked down at her feet. They were clean and dry, but she still had no shoes and stockings. She could not possibly go upstairs in such a state.

"What happened?" asked Constance, following her gaze.

Susannah explained.

"Oh, dear, the captain will be sure to be suspicious if he sees you like that, and I can't fetch you some more from your room. There isn't time."

Acting quickly, she sat down on one of the hard wooden chairs. Turning her back on them, she began taking off her own shoes and stockings.

"But what will you do?" Susannah asked. "If you are barefoot it will seem just as suspicious."

"I will wear my slippers, and if the captain notices, I will plead bunions," Constance said.

She handed her shoes and stockings to Susannah, then put on her slippers, which were warming by the fire.

"You had better tell Captain Johnson we have returned from a ride," said Oliver to Constance, when she had done. "Bring him to meet us in the sitting-room."

Then, whilst Constance headed towards the library, Susannah and Oliver went into the sitting-room. It seemed placid, a place of warm contentment, and was the perfect setting for the act of innocence they were about to perform. The fire was glowing in the fireplace, whilst the candles bathed the room in a warm glow. The clock ticked quietly in the corner. Susannah sat on the sofa and arranged her skirts around her, whilst Oliver sat next to her, assuming a pose of relaxed ease.

"Here," said Susannah, handing him some of the engravings Mrs. Wise had sent to her. "These are from *Ackermann's Repository*. We are choosing new furniture, as we are going to refurbish the house. We have just decided against a lacquered cabinet, and we are contemplating a new set of chairs."

There was time for nothing more. There came the sound of the library door opening, and voices could be heard in the hall, then the sitting-room door opened and Captain Johnson entered.

"Captain Johnson, you are here again," said Susannah. Her tone of voice was mild, but with a hint of reproof. It said, As I am a lady I will receive you with all due courtesy, but you have made a false charge against my fiancé, and you are not welcome here. "How may we help you?"

The captain's eyes flew to Oliver and then back again. He had obviously thought Constance was lying when she had said that Oliver had returned, and his face was a picture of confusion, anger and chagrin.

"You were out," he said. "Where? May I ask," he added belatedly, as though realizing how rude his outburst had been. But his eyes were shrewd and it was clearly no idle question.

"If it is any business of yours—which, however, I doubt—we were riding," she said coolly.

"Your housekeeper said you were out walking," he returned sharply.

"To begin with, yes," said Susannah. "Then Oliver suggested we take the horses and go for a ride."

"In the dark?" he sneered.

"In the starlight," returned Susannah. "Have you ever ridden in the starlight, Captain? You should, you know. It is the best way to see the land and the sea, when they are bathed in the silvery glow. It is very romantic."

The captain's mouth set in a grim line. "No doubt." He turned to Oliver. "You are busy, I see, sir," he said, glancing at the engravings on Oliver's lap.

"Choosing furniture," said Oliver. "My fiancée has a mind to refurbish the house before our marriage. She has been showing me some engravings of the styles she finds particularly attractive. A friend of hers has kindly sent them from town. There are some very fine tables and chairs to be had in London."

"Tables and chairs?" said the captain, with barely concealed contempt. "I should have thought boats and guns were of more interest to you."

"Really? How extraordinary," said Oliver, looking the captain in the eye and challenging him to contradict him.

The captain's face went red. He fought hard to suppress his anger, but he was clenching his fists by his side.

"And where did you go on your ride?" he demanded.

"We rode inland," said Susannah. "We were planning a garden. The grounds are neglected at the moment, but all that will soon change. I'm thinking of a knot garden. What is your opinion, Captain? It is rather old-fashioned perhaps, but as the house is old, I thought it would go very well."

"I know nothing about gardening, ma'am," he snapped.

"Then you should take it up. It is very healthful, and very relaxing. It would be the perfect antidote to your professional life," she said calmly.

The captain's face was like thunder.

"And what about your friends?" he asked. "Mr. Catling and Mr. Owen, if I am not mistaken. Did they go riding, too?"

"No, but they kindly offered to see to our horses when we returned. They are in the stables."

"A popular occupation," sneered Captain Johnson. "If I'm not mistaken, *you* were in the stables the last time I called. I thought you had a groom to see to such things . . . but perhaps, he is in the stables with them?"

There was something almost satisfied in the captain's voice, and Susannah felt Oliver stiffen at her side. What had happened to Kelsey? she wondered. In all the confusion she had forgotten about him, but he had been missing since they had heard the shot on the beach. He could be injured or dead. And if he was injured, he could be a captive of the captain's.

Oliver spoke levelly, and if not for the fact that she could feel his body hard against her own, she would have thought he was relaxed and at ease.

"He is . . . indisposed," he said.

"Is he now?" enquired the captain. His frustration had disappeared and he was growing more and more confident. "He's in bed, I take it?"

"No. I sent him to the apothecary. He will not be back tonight."

"Really? That's interesting. Very interesting. Because I have him right here."

He jerked his head towards one of his men, and Susannah leant closer to Oliver, taking some comfort from his body heat. The soldier went out, but returned a minute later with Kelsey. Then he has been caught, thought Susannah with a sinking feeling.

But then she realized that Kelsey did not have the look of a captured man. Though his rough clothes were dirty with the crossing and his hair was tangled, his head was up and there was a smile playing around his lips.

"Now how do you explain that?" asked the captain.

"I find that hard to explain," said Oliver softly. "Very hard indeed."

AMANDA GRANGE

"Do you? Your groom's an interesting man. He's been telling us some very interesting things about you." Captain Johnson suddenly dropped his polite air. "The time for pretending has gone. We know exactly what you're doing here, Bristow, and Duchamp wants it stopped."

"Duchamp?" enquired Oliver.

"It's no use playing the innocent with me. I suspected you as soon as I heard rumours of three men living alone in an isolated house, so I set out to make sure. A direct approach didn't work, so I tried something more subtle. A bribe to your servant was all it took to confirm your activities."

"This is all very interesting, Captain, but I don't know what you're talking about," said Oliver, with a hint of impatience in his voice. "My fiancée and I have listened to you politely, but if you have nothing intelligible to say then you must excuse us, as we have plans to make."

"I know all about your sailing over to France and breaking men out of prison before bringing them back to the safety of England."

"And who has been telling you this nonsense?" asked Oliver with a sigh. "I do hope it isn't my groom. You should know, Captain, that he has an unfortunate penchant for gambling, and he cannot support the habit on the wages I give him. If you've paid for this information, then I suggest you ask for your money back—although I doubt if you'll get

246

it. Unless I'm much mistaken he's already given everything you paid him to his creditors. But don't take my word for it. If you think there are members of the French nobility hidden in the house, you are welcome to search it. But please do so quietly."

He turned his attention back to the engravings. Taking her lead from him, Susannah turned the pages of the book and then pointed to one of the engravings.

"The Chippendale chairs, I think, for the dining-room," she said. "They are so much more elegant than the ones we have at present. The ones with the shield back, I think, or do you prefer the lyre back chairs?"

"You think you've outsmarted me, but you're mistaken," said the Captain. "We'll find them, wherever they are."

"Perhaps when you do so, you will bring them into the sitting-room," said Susannah. "The French have excellent taste, and they can advise us on what sort of furniture to buy."

The Captain's face grew red with anger. "You'd better be right about this," he said, turning to Kelsey.

"I am," said Kelsey. "There were seventeen people in the boat. They all came ashore. I don't know where he's hiding them, but they have to be here somewhere. He must have known about another passage into the house and brought them in through that."

"Then all we have to do is look." He turned back to

Oliver. "You'd save us all a great deal of time if you'd tell us where they are. If not, we might damage the house in our zeal," he said menacingly.

"If you do, my lawyer will hear of it," returned Susannah.

"Hah!" said the captain. "You, you," he said, pointing to two of the soldiers, "wait outside the door. The rest of you, come with me."

The militia filed out of the room, followed by the captain and Kelsey.

"Oh, Kelsey," said Oliver, as Kelsey was about to step out of the door. "I am sure you have guessed by now, but in case you haven't, your services will no longer be required."

Kelsey threw him a sneering look and departed.

"So it was Kelsey," said Susannah, when they had gone. "I never imagined for a minute he would betray you."

"Neither did I," said Oliver. "I thought it was one of the villagers, or possibly Jim."

"Jim?" asked Susannah in surprise.

"Yes. It never occurred to me that the traitor was closer to home."

"Why did he do it, do you think?"

"Money. I wasn't lying when I said he has a gambling habit. He does. I've helped him out on a number of occasions when he was being pursued by his creditors, but he will always need more."

"And he repays you by turning on you?"

"Not everyone is as trustworthy as you," he said, turning towards her. "You saved us tonight, Susannah. Without your help, the last group of *émigrés* would have been returned to France and killed, and Edward, James and I would have suffered a similar fate."

"I did it gladly," she said.

"I know." He looked round the sitting-room. "There is nothing I will regret when we leave here on Tuesday. Nothing except you." His look intensified, and he put his hand up to brush her cheek. As the back of his hand grazed her skin she shivered, and he drew her into his arms and kissed her.

At last he drew away.

"When I came to Harstairs House, I was a disillusioned man," he said, looking into her eyes. "I had lost my faith in human nature. I had seen a woman whip a man for being poor, and I had seen men murdering each other for saying 'Long live the King.' I came home, sickened by what I had seen, but instead of finding balm for my spirit, the things I saw here sickened me even more. I saw husbands and wives having affairs behind each other's backs; moreover, I was approached by a number of women intent on using me as part of their deceptions. I saw children wishing for their parents' death so that they could inherit their fortunes; and brothers and sisters turning against each other for the sake of money. It seemed that everywhere I looked I saw betrayal. And then I met you, and I discovered that trust and loyalty still existed. I wanted to call you my friend—until I kissed you, and knew friendship would never satisfy me. I love you, Susannah."

He slid from the sofa on to one knee.

"I told the captain we were betrothed and it was not true, but I want to make it true. Susannah, will you be my wife?"

Susannah could barely speak. She loved him so deeply that she could not remember a time when she had not loved him, and to know that he loved her in return filled her with joy. And to know that he wanted her to be his wife . . .

"Yes, Oliver, I will."

He smiled, and it lit his face. His blue eyes gazed into her own. He took her chin between his finger and thumb, and then he kissed her.

Susannah did not want it to end. It felt so wonderful that she wanted it to go on for ever, but at last he let her go.

"We must be married soon," he said, sitting beside her again. "Shall it be here, or on my estate, or in London?"

"In London, I think," said Susannah. "I would like my great aunt's friend, Mrs. Wise, to be present. She is the closest I have to a family."

"Very well then, it shall be in London."

"It's hard to believe I have been here a month, and that I will be leaving tomorrow. Mr. Sinders will be calling for me in his coach," she said. "I will be going to his office to begin with, to finalize the details of my inheritance, and then I will be going on to Mrs. Wise's house." She hesitated, then asked, "Will you carry on with your rescue work, once we are married?"

"No. I told you once before that I was not afraid, and it was true. But now I am afraid, because now I have something to lose. There are other men who will take over and help those in need, but now I want to spend my time with you. I've had enough of bloodshed. Once I have helped the *émigrés* we rescued tonight, taking them to their safe houses, then I will join you in London and my days of adventuring will be done."

Susannah thought of the people in the wash house.

"The captain won't find them, will he?"

"No, my love, he won't. They are too well hidden for that. He might leave men posted outside the gate for a few days, with perhaps a few posted on the coast, and we might have to delay their journey onwards, but he will not be able to stay here for ever and as soon as he leaves I will be able to finish my mission."

"Even so, I will be happier once he has left the house."

"As will we all."

They fell into a companionable silence, broken only by

the shifting of the coals in the fire. Susannah leant her head on Oliver's shoulder and he slid his arm round her as she lost herself in dreams of the happiness to come.

She was finally roused from her happy musings by the sound of footsteps in the hall, marching away from the sitting-room door, and then came the sound of the front door opening and closing. She sat up straight, moving a little way away from Oliver, and a minute later Constance entered the room.

"They've gone," she said.

"Oh, thank goodness," said Susannah, heaving a sigh of relief.

"I asked Captain Johnson if he'd taken his leave of you, but he didn't reply. Instead, he pushed past me and stormed out of the house. He was very annoyed. But at least he has gone. It is not all good news, though, I'm afraid." She turned to Oliver. "He had your groom with him. He seemed to have arrested him."

"Good," said Oliver.

"Good?" asked Constance in surprise. "I don't understand. . . ."

She looked from one to the other of them.

"I must find Edward and James, and tell them the militia have gone," said Oliver. "Can you explain?"

Susannah nodded. "I will tell Constance everything, never fear."

He kissed her on the cheek, then left her alone in the room with Constance.

"Explain?" asked Constance. "Don't tell me there is more that I don't know?"

"Unfortunately, there is. I think you had better sit down."

Constance looked surprised, but sat down nevertheless, and Susannah told her the full story.

"Kelsey betrayed them?" asked Constance in surprise. "Oh my! And he seemed so nice."

Susannah nodded. "I know. He had been with Oliver for some time, but he had been overtaken by gambling fever and he needed money. And so he betrayed his friends."

Constance shook her head. "This is a dreadful affair."

"It is. But it is over . . . or, at least, almost. Oliver and his friends have carried out their last mission from this house. But now, I think we had better see to our guests." She stood up. "They might have to stay here for a few days, until it is safe for them to leave, but Oliver and his friends will stay with them, and see them on their way."

"I wonder if we can make up the bedrooms," said Constance.

"I don't think it will be a good idea for them to sleep upstairs, in case Captain Johnson returns. I think they must stay in the wash house. But we will take them some more blankets and bolsters to help make their stay more pleasant."

"Mr. Bristow is such a wonderful man," said Constance. "Imagine, risking his life to go and rescue his fellow men from the revolution. You are very lucky to be betrothed to him."

"Yes," said Susannah, with a happy smile spreading across her face. "I am."

CHAPTER THIRTEEN

Susannah rose early the following morning, whilst the sky was still dark. She had been tired from her turbulent evening, but she had been too excited to sleep. She was going to marry Oliver!

She washed quickly, before donning a blue open gown and a cream petticoat. After fastening her bodice, she threw a shawl round her shoulders to keep out the cold, then she picked up her candle and went downstairs.

The house was quiet. If she had not known better, she would never have guessed that seventeen people were in the wash house, recovering from their dreadful ordeal. The kitchen was a picture of tranquillity. The brass pans were burnished and were glowing in the firelight, for the kitchen fire was kept in overnight. Susannah lit the candles and then set the kettle over the fire. She glanced at the dresser. It was still pushed across the wash house door. She was not strong enough to move it herself, but it would be pushed aside as soon as the gentlemen arrived.

There was the sound of footsteps coming across the yard, and just as she was going to open the door, thinking it must be Jim with the milk, it opened, and Oliver entered the room, closely followed by Edward.

"You are up early," she said, surprised that they had already been outside.

"We wanted to see if it would be safe to get the *émigrés* away before first light. It will be easier to move them under cover of darkness," said Oliver.

"And is it?" she asked.

"No. At least not yet. The captain's still suspicious. He's left guards, as we suspected he might, two at the gate and two on the cliffs. We will have to delay our departure for a while. Luckily, there is enough food in the house to last for another few days. It will give the *émigrés* a chance to rest and build up their strength."

"And it will give us a chance to replace our horses," said Edward, closing the door behind him.

Susannah looked at him in surprise.

"When we got to the stables this morning, we found them empty," he explained. "Our horses had gone."

"But how . . . ?" asked Susannah.

The two men threw off their greatcoats.

"It's possible Johnson took them to hinder us, and equally possible it was a last act of spite on Kelsey's part," said Edward. "I don't suppose I'll ever see Caesar again. I've had that horse since it was born. I bred it myself," he said with a sigh. Then he rallied. "But it's a setback, nothing more." He glanced at the dresser. "We had better push that aside."

The two gentlemen moved the dresser whilst Susannah continued preparing breakfast. She was soon joined by Constance, who raided the larder for food to give their hungry guests.

"I'm afraid there will not be enough chocolate for everyone," she said. "Our supplies are running low. And there will not be enough rolls. I baked yesterday, but we had to feed everyone when they arrived."

"Never mind, we have other things," said Susannah, following her into the larder and taking down eggs, ham and sausages. "Will James be joining us?" she asked, as she returned to the kitchen.

"Later," said Oliver. "He's gone down to the shore to see if the captain has left any guards in the cove. If not, we might be able to get some of the *émigrés* away in the boat. He might be some time, though, and he would not want us to wait for him."

Susannah glanced at the children, who were hungry, and said, "Very well."

She and Constance began cooking the food and then handing it out. It was an odd assortment of ham, sausages, eggs, cake, fish, cheese and bread, with drinks of tea, ale or milk, but it was evidently very welcome to the *émigrés*, who had languished in prison before crossing the Channel, and who were grateful for anything wholesome. Some of them remained in the wash house, whilst others ate in the kitchen, telling Susannah and Constance of the hardships they had endured. There was a surreptitious nudging when everyone had eaten their fill, and one of the Frenchwomen stepped forward.

"We would like to thank you for everything you 'ave done for us," she said.

"You are very welcome," said Susannah.

She and Constance set about washing the empty plates, helped by some of the Frenchwomen who were rested enough to assist them, but then they could do no more to help, for they had to attend to their own affairs. Their month at Harstairs House was over, and Mr. Sinders would be calling for them shortly. They must be ready to leave when he arrived.

"I can't believe we've been here a month," said Constance, as they went upstairs. "It seems like no time at all since we first arrived."

Susannah agreed. Little had she known that her month at Harstairs House would contain so much that was exciting, perilous and wonderful. And now her life was to get even better, for Oliver was to join her in London.

She left Constance on the landing and went into her bedchamber. She would miss it. She had grown used to its ancient four poster bed, and its heavy washstand with its delicate porcelain bowl. Most of all, she had grown used to its view of the sea. But she was not leaving for ever, she reminded herself. She and Oliver had not yet discussed where they would live when they were married, but she knew they would spend at least part of the year at Harstairs House.

She must remember to give him Mrs. Wise's direction, she thought, as she went over to the wardrobe and took out her few gowns, before folding them and putting them neatly in her portmanteau. She would have to make her final arrangements with him, deciding when he was to call.

Her thoughts were disturbed by the sound of wheels crunching on gravel, and looking out of the window she saw that Mr. Sinder's coach was bowling up the drive. She made haste to pack her last few things and then, donning her outdoor clothes, she closed her portmanteau, picked it up and went downstairs. She had only to take her leave of Oliver, and then she would be on her way.

~ ~ ~

"So it's agreed," said Edward, as he and Oliver finished making their plans in the kitchen. They were sitting at the kitchen table in their shirt sleeves, one on either side of it. "We will wait until the soldiers give up and go away, and then we will walk the *émigrés* across the cliffs. We will have a wagon waiting for them a few miles away, and from there we can take them to safe houses around the country."

"Yes," said Oliver. He paused, and then, leaning back in his chair, he said, "Edward, there's something I have to tell you."

Edward looked at him enquiringly.

"When you move on to a new base, I will not be coming with you."

"Ah." Edward gave a ghost of a smile. "I see. It's because of Susannah?"

"Yes. I'm in love with her," said Oliver simply.

Edward gave a rare smile. "I know," he said.

"Is it so obvious?" asked Oliver in surprise.

"Yes, my friend, it is. You have been haunted recently by some dark secret, and it has made you hard and remote, but ever since meeting Susannah you have started to come back to life. Besides, you are clearly a man in love. You can do nothing these days but smile!"

Oliver laughed. "I know. Everywhere I turn, I see only hope and promise." Then he sobered a little. "And that is why I can't risk my life any more."

Edward said, "I understand. You will be marrying in Cornwall?"

"No. In London. Susannah has no parents, but she has a friend in London and she would like her to be there. Both you and James must come to the wedding as well. I would like you to be my groomsmen."

"Nothing would give me greater pleasure, and I'm sure James will feel the same." He clasped Oliver by the hand. "I'm very glad for you."

"You don't mind me leaving you like this?"

"No. Your time for helping others has passed. Now you need to think of your own life. She's a brave woman, Oliver. You're lucky to have found her. Keep hold of her."

"I intend to," said Oliver.

He stood up, just as the door opened and James entered the room.

"What's this?" asked James, removing his hat and throwing his caped great coat on to a chair.

"You're just in time to congratulate me," Oliver said. "I have asked Susannah to be my wife, and she has said yes."

~ ~ ~

Susannah descended to the hall, with Constance beside her.

"You go on ahead," she said, as she heard the coach pull to a halt outside the door. "Tell Mr. Sinders I will be out shortly. I must say goodbye to Oliver, and give him Mrs. Wise's direction so that he can join us in London. I will be with you soon."

"Of course," said Constance. "Here, let me take your portmanteau. The coachman can be tying it to the roof."

Susannah relinquished her portmanteau, then, whilst Constance went out to the coach, she went to find Oliver. The thought of their parting cost her no more than a brief pang, for it would only be of a short duration. In a few days time they would be reunited in London, and then . . . and then the rest of her life could begin.

As she went down the stone steps leading to the kitchen she heard voices. She sighed. She had hoped for a few minutes alone with Oliver, but it sounded as though Edward and James were with him, so she must put a good face on it.

She heard James saying, "What's this?" as she went along the corridor and then Oliver saying, "You're just in time to congratulate me. I have asked Susannah to be my wife, and she has said yes."

She smiled. *My wife.* How good those words sounded!

"Oliver, no." James's words surprised her. "I've said nothing until now because I believed you when you said you knew where to stop, but I can't let you go through with this. When you first decided to make her fall in love with you I thought it a good joke—"

Joke? thought Susannah, the smile falling from her face.

"But that was before I knew her. Oliver, she's done nothing but help us. She saved us from the militia, and if not for her we could be dead. I can't stand by any longer. You have to put an end to this farce, now, before you do any more harm. To ask her to marry you simply because you overheard her saying she wouldn't marry you if her life depended on it is cruel. Break it off with her. Tell her you can't let her tie herself to a man who's constantly putting himself in danger. Allow her a way out of the situation with her pride and her dignity intact, but don't let this charade go on any longer."

She stopped in the doorway, aghast.

"If you don't," went on James, "I tell you frankly, I will." He broke off as he saw her. "Susannah!" he exclaimed, his look one of dismay.

She stared at him, white-faced, and then at Oliver as he turned round to face her.

"A *charade?*" she said in horror.

"Susannah . . ." said Oliver.

His voice roused her from the horror that had gripped her. She turned and made her way back along the corridor and up the stairs. She scarcely saw where she was going as the terrible scene replayed itself in her mind: James's shocked face, and Oliver turning slowly . . . the back of his head, with its wild locks of long hair, the side, with its powerful profile. . . .

She had thought he loved her, but it had been nothing but a charade. His feelings had been a pretence as a cruel revenge for saying she would never marry him. It had been a deliberate and cold-blooded deception. Every time he had looked at her, or touched her, or kissed her, it had all been a sham.

She crossed the hall and went out of the door. Constance was standing next to the coach, waiting for her. She could not speak of it to anyone, not even Constance. Not yet. And so she hid her feelings deep and pretended that nothing had happened.

"Are you ready?" she asked, marvelling at how calm her voice was.

"Yes," said Constance.

"Then let us be off."

She climbed into the coach and greeted Mr. Sinders. He returned her greeting as she and Constance settled themselves, then the coachman folded up the step, closed the door, climbed on to his box and the coach pulled away.

"Oh, look, there is Mr. Bristow," said Constance, just when Susannah had managed to gain some semblance of calm. "He is running after us."

Mr. Sinders raised his eyebrows. "Perhaps we had better stop," he said.

"No!" said Susannah vehemently.

Constance looked at her in surprise.

Susannah forced herself to be calm. "I'm sure it's nothing important," she said.

"If you say so . . ." said Constance doubtfully, as the coach picked up speed and bowled down the drive.

Mr. Sinders was apparently oblivious to the tension in the coach.

"Well," he began, "if you give me your word you have not left the estate I will be satisfied you have fulfilled the terms of the will, Miss Thorpe. Once we reach my offices in London, I will be able to give you the full details of your inheritance, and as soon as the relevant documents have been signed, I will hand it over to you."

"You are very kind," she said mechanically. "I give you my word I have not left. I would like to thank you for everything you have done for me. I am looking forward to inheriting. It will be wonderful."

But she was not thinking of her inheritance. She was thinking of every minute she had spent with Oliver, and remembering every brush of his lips. Her hand tingled with the memory, and so did her mouth. It had felt so real. . . .

But it had not been real.

~ ~ ~

Oliver cursed as the coach pulled away from him, and at last he had to let it go. He stood looking after it, feeling full of dismay. The horses had gone, and without them he could not catch the coach. He would have to hire an equipage, the fastest the neighbourhood could provide, and make for

London. Once there, he would call on Susannah and explain everything. When he had her in his arms, he knew he could make her understand. James's words had been unfortunate, nothing more. He would tell her everything, reassure her of his love. All he had to do was follow her to Mrs. Wise's house, and everything would be well. But then a sick feeling swept over him. His stomach clenched, and a coldness settled on his heart, because he did not know where Mrs. Wise lived.

CHAPTER FOURTEEN

The journey seemed interminable to Susannah. Constance and Mr. Sinders were both quiet, leaving her alone to her thoughts. If only they had been happier. But instead they tormented her. She thought of every time Oliver had touched her, and every time he had spoken to her, and she felt her heart sink as she realized it had all been a sham. But no good would come of thinking about it, she told herself. She must do her best to put it out of her mind.

She turned her attention to the fields and villages as they rolled by. She joined Constance and Mr. Sinders in commenting on the inns they stopped at along the way, as they took refreshment whilst the horses were changed, and after a long and tiring journey they finally reached London.

Her spirits were low, but she told herself if Oliver could play such a cruel joke, then he was not worthy of her love. She must put him out of her mind, she told herself bracingly. She would have plenty of things to distract her in London, and she would be ungrateful indeed if she wasted another thought on a man who was not worthy of her love. But although her head had no difficulty with this edict, her heart found it hard to apply.

Nevertheless, she looked out of the window as the coach threaded its way through the streets, and made herself take an interest in the assortment of vehicles they passed, from brewers' carts to phaetons, and from curricles to coaches. She noticed a ragged urchin running along the side of the street with a scrawny dog beside him, whilst a smart lady dressed in a blue pelisse and feathered hat was walking along on the arm of a dapper gentleman. A footman was carrying a pile of boxes, and a baker was walking along with a tray of bread on his head. It was the sort of scene that should have gladdened her heart, but even the sight of a young boy riding a pedestrian curricle could not make her smile. The coach finally rolled to a halt in a respectable neighbourhood.

"This is my office," said Mr. Sinders, with dry pride.

The coachman opened the door and let down the step, and Susannah climbed out. She looked up at the building in front of her, telling herself that she must take an interest in it, for Mr. Sinder's sake if not her own. It was modest in size, but it exuded an air of confidence. The door knocker was brightly polished and the paint was fresh. Steps led up to the door, and Mr. Sinders escorted her up to the door. A narrow corridor led to a comfortable office, and she was soon seated opposite Mr. Sinders, whilst Constance was entertained in an ante-room by a junior clerk.

"Might I offer you some ratafia before we begin?" asked Mr. Sinders.

"Thank you," said Susannah.

She was tired after the journey, and she knew the drink would revive her.

After she had taken some refreshment, Mr. Sinders brought out various legal documents and explained in full the terms of Mr. Harstairs's will. Not only had Mr. Harstairs left her Harstairs House and £100,000, he had also left her a number of smaller properties and some bonds besides. Susannah listened carefully to everything Mr. Sinders had to say, and realized that she was wealthy beyond her wildest imaginings. But the vista of new gowns, boxes at the opera and sundry entertainments that opened out before her afforded her no pleasure, because the one thing she really wanted, she had lost. Worse still, she had never really had it.

She turned her attention back to Mr. Sinders. He was telling her about bonds and property, jewels and shares.

"Mr. Harstairs invested wisely," Mr. Sinders said. "He spread his interests, and saw a healthy return on almost everything he bought."

She forced herself to concentrate until Mr. Sinders had finished.

"Thank you for everything you have done for me," said Susannah.

"It is my job," he remarked.

"Even so, you have been at pains to explain everything to me, and I am grateful for it."

"If you have any further questions about your inheritance, I hope you will not hesitate to ask," he said.

"I will be sure to."

She stood up, and he showed her out of his office. She collected Constance from the ante-room and the two ladies took their leave.

"It has been a pleasure to see you again," said Mr. Sinders, as he escorted the two ladies to the coach and handed them in personally.

Once it had rolled away, he went back to his office in a thoughtful mood. Mr. Harstairs had had such high hopes, but it seemed they had come to nothing. Miss Thorpe had made no mention of Mr. Bristow; indeed, she had seemed anxious to get away from him, and Mr. Sinders was not surprised. As a lawyer, he valued bonds and shares and property. Such things were tangible and easily understood.

More volatile matters were best ignored, he felt. But Mr. Harstairs had been adamant.

"I want to give her more than money," he had said, whilst sitting in Mr. Sinders's office not two months before. "I've had property, and look where it's got me."

"To a very comfortable position, if I may say so," Mr. Sinders had remarked.

"A man's not comfortable without a woman," Mr. Harstairs had said, shaking his head. "I should have taken me a bride. There was a woman, once—well, you know. It was Susannah's Great Aunt Caroline. She had a face like an angel, but I was a stupid young thing in those days and I let her go. It was all over something or nothing. She saw me with another woman, and when she asked me about it, instead of telling her it was my old neighbour, I told her she ought to trust me, then got on my high horse and rode it out of the country."

"Doing very well for yourself in the process," Mr. Sinders had reminded him. "Your ventures were singularly successful, and brought you a comfortable, indeed a wealthy, life."

"Oh, yes, 'til the revolutionaries got hold of me and damned near killed me, just because I said I didn't give a fig for their revolution. If not for Oliver Bristow showing up and rescuing me, I'd have been long gone. Once I got back home, I gave him money and a lease on Harstairs

House, so he could carry on with his rescuing. But there's something wrong with that boy. It's eating him up, and if it ain't sorted out soon, it'll be too late. So I'm going to throw 'em at each other, and see what happens."

Mr. Sinders had pointed out that Miss Thorpe might have a former attachment.

"In that case, I'll say she can marry in a month and inherit everything. If there's anyone she's a fancy for, she'll marry him straight away."

"And Mr. Bristow, being of an adventurous disposition, might not suit a quiet governess."

"Quiet? Mebbe. But if she's anything like Caroline she'll be full of pluck. Tell her the house is haunted. If she can take on ghosts, she can take on Bristow. But don't tell her she'll find him there. I don't want her deciding not to go. And if they get married, Sinders, give 'em this. It's a letter, wishing 'em well."

"It's most irregular. . . ."

"Good! Because regular I ain't. Nor is Bristow. Nor, I'll wager, is Miss Thorpe. Look to it, Sinders. My health ain't what it should be. I ain't going to be here much longer, and I want to do what I can for 'em."

It had all come to nothing, of course, thought Mr. Sinders drily. Affairs of the heart always did. It was far better to put faith in solid things like property.

He poured himself a glass of Madeira, and consoled

himself with the thought that although Mr. Harstairs might have been singularly unsuccessful at providing Susannah with a husband, he had been successful in providing her with more tangible assets.

Yes, he thought, as he sipped his Madeira, it was money and property that counted in the end.

~ ~ ~

Susannah's thoughts were of a completely different nature. As the coach pulled away from Mr. Sinders's office and embarked on the last part of its journey she looked out of the window, but she did not see the London streets in the gathering gloom. Instead, she saw Harstairs House, and flashes of all the things that had happened there: her meeting with Oliver, their encounter in the attic, their kiss on the cliffs, their boat ride . . . As she realized what she was doing, she upbraided herself and told herself she should not be thinking of him. She tried hard to think of other things, and had almost succeeded in putting him out of her mind when Constance unwittingly destroyed her hard work by mentioning him.

"Are you going to tell Mrs. Wise about your engagement straight away, or are you going to wait until she has met Mr. Bristow?" Constance asked.

Susannah did not want to talk about it, but she knew it could no longer be avoided. She would have to tell Constance sooner or later, and it would be better if she revealed the truth before they reached Mrs. Wise's house.

"There is no engagement," she said, speaking in a matter-of-fact tone and trying not to let her feelings show. "I am afraid I was deceived in Mr. Bristow. He overheard me telling you I wouldn't marry the tenant if my life depended on it. It was on our first evening here. We were in the sitting-room, and had just discovered the house was occupied, if you remember. You thought Mr. Harstairs might have arranged it deliberately, so that Mr. Bristow and I could meet and fall in love, and I said that I would never marry him."

"Yes, I remember," said Constance, perplexed.

"It challenged him, so he set out to make me fall in love with him."

"I can't believe it," said Constance, taken aback. "He always seemed such an honourable gentleman. Are you sure, Susannah? Could there not have been some mistake?"

"No. There is no mistake. I heard it with my own ears. James was berating him for it as I went down into the kitchen. I had gone to take my leave of him. Oliver was telling James that he had asked me to marry him, and James told him things had gone too far. All this time, I thought he had feelings for me," she said, unable to keep a tremor out of her voice. "But he was only interested in revenge."

"My poor, dear Susannah," said Constance.

She took Susannah's hands between her own and held them comfortingly.

"I would rather you said nothing of this to Mrs. Wise," said Susannah, recovering herself. "I did not mention Mr. Bristow to her, and she has no need to know anything about him."

"Of course not, if you would rather I didn't," Constance assured her.

The coach turned a corner and then began to slow. It finally rolled to a halt. Susannah looked out of the window. She had never visited Mrs. Wise before, and did not know what kind of residence to expect.

The house in front of them was smart, but not too large. It was well kept, with shiny black railings and sparkling sash windows. Lighted flambeaux were set at the bottom of the steps to ward off the coming darkness. The coachman opened the door and let down the step. Susannah climbed out, followed by Constance. The coachman lifted the ladies' scant luggage out of the coach, and then went up the steps and knocked on the door. It was opened almost immediately by an imposing butler who bowed the two ladies inside before leading them upstairs to the drawing-room.

As the drawing-room door opened, Susannah caught sight of duck-egg blue walls, an Aubusson carpet in shades of blue and red, a quantity of gilded furniture and an abundance of mirrors, which reflected the candlelight and made the room almost as bright as day. And rising from an elegant sofa was a round, cheerful woman with grey hair and twinkling eyes, dressed in an open gown of amber satin. A froth of lace spilled from each of her three-quarter-length sleeves. Rings covered her fingers, and a cap was set on her powdered head.

"Susannah, I'm glad to see you, my dear," she said, taking Susannah by the hands and beaming at her. "You look a little pale. But we will soon put some colour in your cheeks."

She cast a critical eye over Constance before seeming satisfied and welcoming her warmly.

"How was your journey?" she said to Susannah, as she helped her to remove her cloak.

"Very pleasant," said Susannah mechanically.

Mrs. Wise's eyes twinkled.

"By which you mean the roads were abominable, the coach was intolerable and the length interminable! I know, my dear, I have journeyed into the West Country on occasion, and I am sure you must be black and blue. The potholes in those roads! But I mean to make sure you enjoy your stay. I have all sorts of entertainments planned. We will need to be quiet at first, of course, whilst you have some new clothes made, but it should not take too long. The modiste's do not have too much work in December."

Susannah made herself smile. She would enjoy her

time in London, she told herself, with all its distractions of museums and shops, parks and assemblies. She would go to every party, laugh at every pleasantry and accept every compliment, until she had driven Oliver from her mind.

"What a stroke of luck, inheriting a fortune," Mrs. Wise went on. "Your aunt would have been so pleased. She always wanted a good marriage for you, but she thought of nothing better than a rector or a squire. You can aim much higher now. We will have you settled before the end of the summer, I am sure of it, and to a man with a title, as well as ten thousand a year. Our first visit will be to the modiste's tomorrow, and then to the friseur's," she said, studying Susannah critically, as the ladies sat down. "We will have a lot to do if you are to be ready to go to Lady Eldermere's ball on Friday week. It promises to be a splendid occasion, and her son will be there. He is a very eligible gentleman, and is handsome besides. And if he doesn't suit, there are plenty more to choose from. Oh, Susannah, I am so looking forward to this. What fun we are going to have!"

~ ~ ~

Susannah tried to enter into Mrs. Wise's enjoyment over the next few days as she visited modistes, friseurs and milliners, but at night, her dreams went their own way. She was on the cliffs, kissing Oliver, or in the kitchen, melting as he bathed her feet. And then would come her awakening, and her urge to sleep again, so that she could lose herself in her dreams.

Could it have been a mistake? she asked herself. But no, how could it? James would not have said such a thing if it had not been true. So she expressed herself delighted with her new gowns, and charmed with her new hats. She exclaimed over her fashionable hairstyle, and enthused over the glossy ringlets that spilled from a high chignon, cascading over her shoulder and down her back. She visited Mr. Sinders on two further occasions, to take his advice on her inheritance, and appointed Constance as her housekeeper at a generous salary. And she expressed herself enchanted with the idea of Lady Eldermere's ball.

The day before the ball, however, there came an event which required all of her fortitude, for whilst she was sitting in the drawing-room with Mrs. Wise, the butler brought in a card.

Mrs. Wise took it and said in surprise, "Mr. Oliver Bristow."

Susannah almost jumped, and hastily buried her face in a book so that her agitation should not be noticed.

"That's strange," said Mrs. Wise, puzzled. "I don't believe I know a Mr. Bristow. Unless . . . unless," she said, with more animation, "he is one of the Northumberland Bristows. Yes, I do believe he is. I remember now." She turned to the butler. "Ask Mr. Bristow to join us."

"No!" said Susannah, jumping up.

Mrs. Wise looked at her in astonishment.

Susannah sat down again hurriedly, angry with herself for having betrayed so much feeling, but she could not face Oliver, especially not here, in Mrs. Wise's drawing-room.

"That is, I am feeling a little unwell," said Susannah. "I am very sorry," she said to Mrs. Wise, "but I don't feel I am equal to receiving visitors."

"My dear, you should have said," remarked Mrs. Wise serenely. She turned to the butler. "Inform Mr. Bristow that I am not at home."

"Very good, ma'am," he said with a bow, and withdrew.

"I'm so sorry," said Susannah. "I didn't mean to spoil your day, but my head . . . I think I should go to my room."

"By all means," said Mrs. Wise kindly, ". . . but not until you have told me what is troubling you."

Susannah's heart began to beat faster.

"I can't think what you mean," she prevaricated.

"I don't know what has happened to you, Susannah, but you have not been yourself since you arrived," said Mrs. Wise. "I have watched you trying to appear interested in your new gowns, but it has been an effort for you, and don't tell me that you have lost your interest in fashion, because I don't believe it. When I used to visit Caroline, you pored over the fashion plates I brought with me. I have said nothing so far because I did not want to distress you, but it can't go on. It has something to do with Mr. Bristow, has it not?"

Susannah made no reply.

"My dear, I have never met Mr. Bristow in my life, and now he comes calling on me. The only attraction of my house can be that you are here. Will you not tell me what is wrong?"

Susannah shook her head, but a few minutes were enough to show her that she owed Mrs. Wise an explanation.

"I knew Mr. Bristow in Cornwall. . . ." she began, and as she started to speak she felt a sense of relief that at last it was out in the open.

"This is very bad," said Mrs. Wise, shaking her head when Susannah had finished. "Very bad indeed. I would not have believed it possible of him. He comes from a very respectable family, and he was properly raised. Now I think of it, I remember his grandparents, too. They were a charming couple. I'm convinced their grandson would never behave in such a way."

"Things happened to him," Susannah said haltingly. "He had some dreadful experiences in France. I believe they changed him."

"You think they made him cruel?"

"I . . ." Susannah shook her head. "I don't know."

"I cannot believe it. If it had just been a question of him making love to you in Cornwall, then perhaps, if he was wholly lost to decency, he might have done so, but here it is a different matter. We are in London now. It is the heart of the civilized world. His behaviour will not go unnoticed. He cannot visit you at my house and expect the world to look the other way if he deceives you. It will affect his reputation."

"I don't believe he cares for his reputation," said Susannah with a sigh. "He will probably not be in London for very long."

Mrs. Wise opened her mouth, as though she was about to argue, and then closed it again. She paused, then said robustly, "Well, whatever the case, he is not making you happy, and that is enough reason for you to look about you and choose someone else. There are plenty of eligible gentlemen in London. At the moment you have no wish to see them. I understand. Your head has accepted the situation but your heart is still with Mr. Bristow. Never fear, that will pass. I will not plague you by introducing you to eligible gentlemen for the moment. I suggest you simply enjoy our outings as a pleasant change from your former life. There will be time enough for you to think of another husband once your heart has mended."

~ ~ ~

Oliver cursed under his breath as the butler informed him that Mrs. Wise was not at home. It had taken him over a week to discover the address of Susannah's hostess, and now that he had done so she had refused to see him. He was seized with an urge to argue, and to force his way into the house if necessary, but there were six footmen in the hall, and he could not force his way past them all. But there were other ways to meet with Susannah. He had only to find out where she went and what she did, and he would be able to speak to her, and explain. He could not lose her, not now, not ever.

He made the butler a stiff bow and turned away from the house, descending the steps and then striding back to his lodgings. As he crossed town his mind was active, planning how he might best see her. He was so engrossed in his thoughts that when he entered his lodgings he did not immediately realize that he was not alone. He had entered his sitting-room and thrown down his hat before seeing that he had a visitor.

James sprang to his feet.

Oliver stopped short. "How did you get in?" he asked. His tone was not welcoming.

"Your landlady let me in." James looked him in the eye. "I told her I had to see you on a matter of business, and asked if I could wait."

Oliver walked across the room and threw himself into a

chair, raising one leg over the arm. "I see. You have come to tell me about the *émigrés*, I take it? Did they get away safely?"

"Yes. We managed to get them all out of Cornwall, and they have now all been established in new homes."

"Good."

"But that is not why I'm here. I had to come and apologize to you," said James, sitting down. "Edward explained everything to me as soon as you ran out of the kitchen. I would have apologized to you straight away, but you didn't come back into the house, and you left the grounds so quickly I didn't have a chance. I'm sorry. I made a mess of things."

"It wasn't your fault," said Oliver briefly. "I'm glad you spoke out. If I had been using Susannah, it's good to know she would have found a champion in you."

"It's generous of you to say so," said James, relaxing a little. "But I haven't come here only for that. I want to make amends. I thought if you'd found out where Susannah was staying I could go to her and explain. I am the one who made the mess. The least I can do is to clear it up."

"No." Oliver shook his head. "It would do no good. She would not believe you." His voice dropped. "I am the only one who can make her believe."

"Then you've been to see her?"

"I tried. But she wouldn't see me."

"Then let me try."

"No. I mean to find a way, and when I do, I intend to tell her the truth. She has to know that what started out as a challenge turned into love."

"And then?" asked James.

"And then," he said, growing pale, "I have to hope she forgives me."

~ ~ ~

Since telling Mrs. Wise of her troubles, Susannah had felt some alleviation of her spirits. She no longer had to pretend to enthuse over fashion plates or the latest style of hat, and she was able to look forward to Lady Eldermere's ball, safe in the knowledge that Mrs. Wise would not introduce her to a succession of potential husbands. When it was time for her to dress she sat down at the dressing table whilst Mrs. Wise's maid piled her hair high on her head, arranging a swathe of ringlets over her left shoulder, before decorating it elegantly yet simply with a single ostrich feather. Then, with the help of the maid, she donned her gown. It was a beautiful creation with a white skirt, padded out with a bustle at the back, and a yellow and white striped bodice. She slipped into a pair of yellow silk shoes and the maid fastened a string of pearls round her neck, then she went downstairs.

Mrs. Wise was already in the hall. She was splendidly

dressed. Her gold silk gown was matched by diamonds at her throat and wrist, and was set off by a powdered wig. To Susannah's eyes the wig looked old-fashioned, but it suited Mrs. Wise, adding a certain dignity to her air. Constance appeared behind her, dressed becomingly in a simple gown of blue cambric. She had resisted Susannah's efforts to provide her with something more luxurious, but had succumbed to the temptation to wear a wig.

"I know it is becoming less fashionable, but without one, at such a splendid gathering, I feel only half dressed," she said.

The maid fastened fur-lined cloaks over the ladies' gowns, then they went out into the December night. The air was crisp, and they hurried across the pavement to Mrs. Wise's elegant carriage.

"You must think about providing yourself with a carriage when you return to Cornwall," said Mrs. Wise, as they took their places and a footman closed the door behind them. "You cannot manage in a country neighbourhood without one. Unless I can persuade you to remain in London, that is."

"Perhaps I might," said Susannah, as they set off.

Harstairs House held painful memories for her, and she no longer looked forward to making her home there. Perhaps London, with its many distractions, would be more agreeable.

It did not take them long to reach Lady Eldermere's street, but then they had to wait in a queue of carriages. The going was slow, and it took some fifteen minutes for them to reach the front. Once there, they stepped out and arranged their skirts before sweeping up the broad steps to the open door. Liveried footmen stood there, resplendent in powdered wigs, and beyond them was a scene of brilliant gaiety. Ladies were colourful in their silk and brocade gowns, fluttering their fans and bobbing their heads as their ostrich feather headdresses swayed and danced. They were accompanied by gentlemen in satin coats and knee breeches, with rings winking from their fingers and lace spilling from their sleeves.

"Oh my!" said Constance, as they ascended the staircase.

"This is wonderful," said Susannah, whilst they waited on the landing until their hostess could greet them.

She looked about her and marvelled over the gilded mirrors and the thick carpet.

"I thought you would like it," said Mrs. Wise. "Ah! Dear Lady Eldermere! Might I present my protégé, Miss Susannah Thorpe?"

Lady Eldermere was an elegant woman built on statuesque lines. She was clothed in a magnificent brocade gown which was open to reveal a silk petticoat, and a powdered wig was set on her head. She held up her lorgnette and surveyed Susannah with interest.

"Caroline's great-niece, aren't you, gal?" she asked.

"That's right."

"You're a credit to her," she said, lowering her lorgnette.

There was time for no more. Lady Eldermere had other guests to greet, and Susannah's party moved on, passing through into the ballroom. Mrs. Wise had promised her she should dance only with elderly gentlemen at the ball, and was true to her word. Susannah found herself partnered by a succession of men old enough to be her father, and to her surprise she found she was enjoying herself. The stately dances were to her liking, and if her partners were not handsome, at least they did not pester her with their attentions. They talked of the size of the room and the splendour of the setting, of her impressions of London and her views on Cornwall, and when they had finished with these topics they complimented her gracefully on her gown and her hair.

Even so, as the evening drew on she became restless. Try as she might, she could not put Oliver completely out of her mind. His face kept intruding on her memory as a hundred small details of their time together occurred to her.

Could there have been some mistake? she asked herself, not for the first time. If not, why would he have visited her? He could hardly have expected to escape unscathed if he had pursued her at Mrs. Wise's house. Society might be more stringent in its standards for young ladies, but it was not entirely devoid of them for gentlemen.

But why would James have said it if it wasn't true?

"Might I have the pleasure of this dance?" came a quavery voice at her side.

Susannah lifted her head to see a gentleman of some eighty years of age, whose eyes were sparkling at her.

"I knew your great aunt, m'dear," he said, as she thanked him and took his hand.

He led her out on to the floor.

"She was a spirited girl," he said with a nostalgic air, as the music began, and he and Susannah performed the stately steps of the dance. "I remember thinking she'd marry Henry Harstairs. He was a mushroom, but he had a way with him, and Caroline always liked strong characters. Although Henry's character was too strong," he said with a sigh. "After their falling out he wouldn't make things right. Instead, he went abroad."

"What was their falling out about?" asked Susannah curiously.

"I don't know. Some misunderstanding, nothing more. Silly to let such a little thing come in the way of their happiness, but so it was. If only they'd talked about it. But they were headstrong, both of them."

Susannah found the noise of the ballroom starting to feel oppressive and she longed for the dance to be over.

Once it was, and her partner had escorted her to the side of the room, she made her excuses, saying she was going in search of the ladies' withdrawing room. She slipped out of the ballroom and into the corridor, looking for a quiet room in which she could retreat from the bright lights and the bustle for a few minutes. At the end of the corridor she found a small room lit only by the crackling flames of a fire. Away from the music and the lights she started to feel better. She would have to go back soon, but she could have a few minutes in which to compose herself. She went in, and walked over to the fireplace. It was a peaceful interlude, and soothed her spirits . . . until she heard the door opening behind her. She turned round, ready to explain her presence, and froze, as she saw that the person standing there was Oliver. He was dressed in blue satin, with a froth of lace at his throat, and his hair was tied back with a dark blue riband, but instead of being confident as he usually was, he was looking strangely vulnerable.

"What are you doing here?" she asked, feeling her limbs begin to tremble, although whether it was with anger or some other emotion she could not tell.

"I came to see you," he said.

"Then you will be disappointed."

He was standing between her and the door.

"I wish to leave," she said.

He did not move. Through the open door she heard

faint strains of music, and the muted laughter of Lady Eldermere's guests.

"Stand aside," she said.

To her relief he took a step to the left.

"If you want to go, I won't stop you," he said.

Her way to the door was now clear. The brilliant light of
the corridor beckoned her. She had only to walk past him
and she could return to the ballroom, putting him behind
her forever.

But something made her hesitate. His pose was so de-
fenceless that it touched something deep inside her. He
could use his strength to detain her, but he was not prepared to do it. He was giving her a choice, to leave or to
remain.

She swallowed. "Very well," she said.

He closed the door. The light of the corridor disappeared. In the dim firelight she could not read his expression and she felt a shiver go through her. She was shut in
with him.

"Susannah . . ." he began haltingly. "Susannah . . . I
have to explain."

She waited, saying nothing.

He took a step towards her and she took a step back.
He stopped.

"When I first met you, and heard you saying that you
wouldn't marry me if your life depended on it, it's true that

I was challenged by it," he began again. "I made up my mind then and there that I would make you want me, so I set out to charm you. But then something happened." His eyes lifted to hers. "I started to find out that you were not like other women, that you were trustworthy, and when I took you in my arms on the cliffs, I realized that I was in as much danger as you were. I decided to withdraw whilst I could. But I found it was impossible. The more I came to know you, the more I came to love you, and I wanted to make you my wife. When I knew you wanted it, too . . ." His mouth lifted, and the candle flame caught the blueness of his eyes ". . . it made my spirits soar. But then came James's remark. It was true once, but a long time ago. To me, it seems a lifetime ago."

He stood there in the soft glow of the fire and candlelight, without moving. "I love you, Susannah. I love you so much it hurts. If you don't believe me . . ." His voice broke, but then he continued, "I offer you my hand and my heart, Susannah. If you want them, they are yours."

"And how am I to know you are being honest with me?" she asked, forcing her limbs to stop trembling. "On the night I arrived at Harstairs House I said I would never marry you. How do I know that making me accept your hand is not your final act of revenge?"

"You don't."

He said nothing more. He did not try and persuade

her, and she knew he could have done. He could have reminded her of all the dangers they had shared. He could
have taken her in his arms and driven all thoughts of everything else out of her mind. But he stood there, unmoving
and vulnerable, isolated and waiting. He had tracked her
down in London, found out where she was staying, tried
to see her whilst she was under the protection of friends,
then followed her to a ball when he could not see her in
any other way. And as she stood there looking at him she
knew he was everything she had ever wanted; and more,
because the worlds he had shown her had been beyond her
experience and even her imagination. And she could have
him . . . if she took a leap of faith.

Could she take it?

She searched her feelings.

Yes, she could. She took a half step towards him, and
he was across the room in the blink of an eye, sweeping her
into his arms and kissing her with all the passion of his soul.
She returned his kiss with fervour.

"I thought I'd lost you," he said, as at last they parted.

"For a time," she returned with a sigh.

"Can you ever forgive me?" he asked, stroking her face
and searching her eyes with his own.

She smiled up at him.

"I already have done."

He put his arms around her and kissed her again, tenderly this time, with all the promise of a lifetime of kisses to come.

Susannah responded—until she heard the click of the door opening.

"You were such a long time, I wondered if you were feeling all right," came a familiar voice. "One of the footmen saw you coming in here. Are you feeling—oh!"

Susannah pulled herself from Oliver's embrace and turned round to see Mrs. Wise, who was looking at Oliver with a formidable expression on her face.

"What is the meaning of this?" she demanded.

"The meaning, dear Mrs. Wise," said Susannah with a happy smile, "is that we are going to be married."

"Ah!" said Mrs. Wise. Her shoulders relaxed and her eyes twinkled. "So *this* is Mr. Bristow!"

Amanda Grange lives in Cheshire, England, and has written many novels including *Darcy's Diary* and *Captain Wentworth's Diary*. Visit her website at www.amandagrange.com.